RED SNOW

RED SNOW

WAYNE D. OVERHOLSER

THORNDIKE
CHIVERS

This Large Print edition is published by Thorndike Press, Waterville, Maine, USA and by AudioGO Ltd, Bath, England.
Thorndike Press, a part of Gale, Cengage Learning.
The text of this Large Print edition is unabridged.
Other aspects of the book may vary from the original edition.
Set in 16 pt. Plantin.

LIBRARY OF CONGRESS CATALOGING-IN-PUBLICATION DATA

Overholser, Wayne D., 1906-1996.
   Red snow / by Wayne D. Overholser. — Large print ed.
    p. cm. — (Thorndike Press large print western)
   ISBN-13: 978-1-4104-3729-7
   ISBN-10: 1-4104-3729-9
   1. Large type books. I. Title.
PS3529.V33R45 2011
813'.54—dc22
                                   2011011209

BRITISH LIBRARY CATALOGUING-IN-PUBLICATION DATA AVAILABLE

Published in 2011 in the U.S. by arrangement with Golden West Literary Agency.
Published in 2011 in the U.K. by arrangement with Golden West Literary Agency.

U.K. Hardcover: 978 1 445 83786 4 (Chivers Large Print)
U.K. Softcover: 978 1 445 83787 1 (Camden Large Print)

Printed in the United States of America
1 2 3 4 5 6 7 15 14 13 12 11

RED SNOW

CHAPTER 1

Rick Proctor, sitting in the back row in the geometry class, felt a tap on his shoulder. He turned his head to see the principal, who motioned toward the door. Rick rose and stepped into the hall. It was then ten minutes before four.

The principal closed the door. He said, "Doc Doan's in my office. He wants to talk to you."

"What about?"

"He didn't say. I have some errands to do so I won't need the office. You go ahead and talk to Doc."

Rick turned toward the principal's office, worried because he couldn't think of any reason the doctor would want to see him — unless his mother was sick. As he went into the office and saw Doc's worried face, he sensed that something was worse than his mother's illness.

The doctor was an old man who had come

to Proctor City shortly after the Civil War. Back in those days the town was little more than a post office, a saloon, and a general store. Doc was short and pudgy, with white hair and a white mustache and a half-chewed cigar tucked into one corner of his mouth. He was a kindly man who was loved by everyone in the county — except Rick's father. Jay Proctor didn't, as far as Rick knew, love anyone.

"Howdy, Rick." Doan motioned to a chair. "Sit down. I apologize for taking you out of class, but I had to talk to you."

"I don't mind leaving geometry," Rick said.

Rick sat down, thinking he had never seen the doctor so upset before. He had watched Doan at times when he was under great stress, but the medico had never shown his feelings as he did now. A muscle throbbed in his cheek like a pulse, and his faded blue eyes were deeply troubled. His hands trembled as he picked up a pencil and began tapping the desk.

"When were you home last?" Doan asked.

"Christmas."

"And this is the last of March," Doan said thoughtfully. "Why don't you go home more often?"

"You know damned well why I don't,"

Rick said, irritated because he knew the question was unnecessary; Doc Doan knew all about his family. Still, he answered out of respect, "I don't get along with pa. It was a mistake to go home when I did."

"But Rainbow is only four miles from here," Doan said. "What are you afraid of?"

"I just don't want to fight with pa," Rick said. "I see ma once in a while when she comes to town and I write to her and she writes to me. Now what in the hell are you quizzing me like this for?"

"I'm not just prying into your affairs." Doan pulled at his mustache for a moment, his gaze on Rick's face, then said, "I thought you could tell me more about what's going on out there. Your mother expects me to do something and I don't know what to do."

He drew an envelope from his inside coat pocket and tossed it on the desk. "I got that this afternoon. Read it."

Rick picked up the letter, noting that it was addressed in his mother's precise handwriting. He pulled the folded sheet of paper from the envelope and opened it.

Rainbow
March 20, 1902

Dear Doctor Doan:

I know I'm imposing on you, but I don't know who else to turn to. I wrote to Sheriff Osmand last week and I have heard nothing from him, so I'm writing to you. Unless someone does something soon to prevent it, Jay is going to have Milt Smith killed. Can you do anything?

Sincerely yours,
Mary Proctor

Rick couldn't say anything for a moment. A sickness began crawling into his belly. What he had feared for months was about to happen. Finally he said, "You know I'm going to marry Ruth Smith, don't you, Doc?"

Doan nodded. "That was why I came to you. You've got a stake in this on both sides. But what can I do?"

"I don't know," Rick said. "What can anybody do with a crazy man?"

"Is your pa that bad?"

"You ought to know," Rick said. "You claim you're never going back to Rainbow."

"I'm not," Doan said, "but Jay cussing me like he did for no reason is not enough to prove he's crazy. A lot of pretty sane men have cussed me in the course of my life."

Rick shrugged his shoulders. "Maybe so, but pa's been crazy ever since the accident that's kept him tied down to that wheelchair of his. He sits in the front room by the window and uses his glasses to study the Smith house. It's too far away to see much, but he does it, and all the time he's hating Milt like I never knew of one man hating another. I guess it's the hate that made him crazy."

Doan rose. "I don't want to keep you any longer, but I thought you might have some idea what I can do. This is over and beyond anything professional for me, but I don't want to see Milt murdered. It could start a bloodbath."

"The only thing I know is to see Osmand," Rick said. "He's not much of a sheriff and he's beholden to pa, just like Judge Callahan. He wouldn't have been elected if pa hadn't supported him. Likely he won't do anything, but he's all we've got."

"I'll see him," Doan said, "but I think you're right about Osmand. We all came out here about the same time, but your pa was a very young man, while me and Callahan and Osmand were a lot older. Jay had the time and ambition to build himself an empire. There aren't too many people around who'd be crazy enough to stand up to Jay Proctor." He picked up his derby and then stood looking at Rick. "You know, I've thought for quite a while that Jay was crazy, but how do you stop him?"

Doan walked out of the office, slapping his derby on his head. Rick returned to the geometry room just as the bell rang. Students filled the hall, some of them hooraying Rick about the principal calling him out of the room, but he ignored them. He stopped at the teacher's desk long enough to write down the next day's assignment, then got his coat and hat and left the building.

Rick shivered as he stepped outside. He buttoned his collar up around his neck and walked faster. A storm was moving in. The air had felt like snow all day. Now the sky was an ominous lead-gray color, and the wind had a bite that cut into a man's bones.

Some of the worst storms Rick had ever seen came in late March. He had heard stories of the Big Die years ago and how it had wiped out ranchers all the way to Canada. It was probably too late in the year for a storm to hang on like that, he thought. Still, it could happen again. Milt Smith didn't have many head of cattle left, but Jay Proctor would be hurt badly, particularly because his foreman, Curly Klein, was a lazy bastard who talked a lot and worked very little.

This was one point where Rick agreed completely with his older brother Barney, but their father was not one to listen when it came to something he'd made up his mind about. He couldn't get out on the range to see for himself what was going on, and he trusted Klein completely. This, Rick told himself sourly, was proof that his father's accident had affected his brains as well as his legs.

He didn't see Monte Bean, one of the Rainbow hands, standing in front of Mrs. Laird's house where he roomed and boarded, until he was almost on top of him. Rick stopped on the board walk ten feet from the gate that opened into Mrs. Laird's yard. Bean's horse was ground-hitched another twenty feet behind him.

Rick stood motionless, his fists clenched. Monte Bean was the last man he wanted to see. Or almost the last. Curly Klein would have been the last, but Bean was Klein's right arm. Last summer when Rick had cowboyed for Rainbow, Bean had made life hell for him. Rick had sworn he'd never

13

work at home again as long as Bean was there.

"Well," Bean said in a belligerent tone, "this is a cold day to have to wait for you to come home."

"Nobody asked you to wait," Rick said. "Why don't you get on your horse and quit waiting?"

"You always were a cocky devil," Bean said, grinning. "I thought we took some of that out of you last summer, but I reckon we didn't."

"Say your piece and git," Rick said.

Bean walked toward him, his muscular arms swinging at his sides. He was older than Rick by ten years, heavier and broader of shoulder, but Rick, who stood an inch over six feet, was taller. He had never fought the man, but he had come close to it, and he would have on at least two occasions during the summer if Barney hadn't been there to step between them.

"All right," Bean said. "I'll say it and you listen good. We've got things running smooth on Rainbow and we aim to keep it that way, but your ma's interfering. She wrote to the sheriff last week. We know because Barry told us he mailed the letter for her.

"We don't know what she said, but we've

got some ideas, so we told Osmand to keep his nose clean. Now she's wrote to Doc Doan, and that's something else again because Doan's a stubborn old goat who don't listen the way Osmand does. This is where you come in. She'll listen to you. Tell her to quit writing letters if she wants to stay healthy."

Rick stared at the man, unable to believe the threat he'd heard. Outraged, he said, "You lay a hand on her and by God, I'll kill you."

Bean laughed, a taunting sound that was aimed at provoking Rick. He took another step forward. He said, "That's tough talk, sonny. Let me give it to you straight. If that bitch of a mother of yours . . ."

Rick hit him, a solid right that rocked Bean's head and drove him back a step. He had been looking for this, but Rick moved faster than he had expected and he didn't get a chance to recover. Rick was on him like a cat, sledging him with rights and lefts and finally getting a hard blow squarely to his nose. It flattened like an overripe plum, blood spurting all over his face.

Bean struck back, but Rick was ducking and weaving, Bean's big fist missed by a fraction of an inch. Bean, angry and frustrated, let out a great bull-like bellow and

15

came at Rick with his head down, his arms outstretched.

Rick kicked him in the crotch. For a moment Bean stood paralyzed with pain, his arms lowered to his sides. Rick hit him on the jaw, a powerful blow that knocked him into the street dust. Rick fell on him, his knees driving wind out of the man, and struck him on one side of the face and then the other, Bean's head rocking back and forth with the blows.

Suddenly Mrs. Laird's screams got through the red haze of fury that possessed Rick. She was tugging at one shoulder and crying, "You've whipped him, Rick. Let him up. Don't murder the man."

Slowly Rick got up off the cowboy and rubbed his skinned knuckles. He said, "Get on your horse, Bean. If I ever hear you say one more word about my mother, I'll come at you with more than my fists."

Bean struggled to his feet and reeled to his horse. His face looked like a piece of raw beef. Blood ran down his chin from his nose and a cut lip, one eye was closed, and both cheeks were black and blue with bruises.

He gripped his saddle horn and stood there a moment, then turned his head to glare at Rick with his one good eye. He said,

"Start wearing your gun, kid. Next time you see me, start shooting, because that's what I'll be doing."

His words were slurred because of his split lip, but Rick understood what he said. Bean stepped into the saddle and rode away, his head tipped forward.

Mrs. Laird moved so she could see Rick's face. "Why, he never touched you, did he?"

"Not this time," Rick said.

"Who was he?"

"Monte Bean, a Rainbow hand."

"A Rainbow hand?" she cried. "You mean one of the men who works for your father came here to beat you?"

"That's what he came for, all right," Rick said. "He was trying to make me stay away from Rainbow, I guess. But I wasn't planning on going home anyway."

"Well, I declare," Mrs. Laird said, puzzled. "I'm going to tell your ma the next time I see her. That man should be fired."

"No, don't tell her," Rick said. "You'll only worry her."

He picked up his geometry book from the board walk. It must have fallen during the fight, but somehow Rick didn't remember.

"Come on in, Rick," Mrs. Laird said, "I'll have supper for you right away."

She was a good woman, who mothered

17

him when he was here, but she was nosy. She'd want to know what had started the fight. He'd tell her Bean had said a bad thing about his mother and let it go at that. Bean had certainly been doing Klein's dirty work for him, and that must mean that Klein had done something he was afraid Rick would discover.

Rick went into the house and walked on back to his room. He tossed his book onto the bed, opened his top bureau drawer, and took out his gun. He hadn't worn it for months, but he knew it was time to start.

CHAPTER 2

Curly Klein stood with his back to the barn and watched Monte Bean ride slowly in, his head down, his shoulders hunched forward, one hand gripping the horn. He was reeling from one side to the other as if he was about to fall out of the saddle.

When Bean reached the barn and reined up, Klein stepped forward and took the reins. "What's the matter with you?" he demanded. Then he saw Bean's face. "My God, man, you look like you just ran into a buzz saw!"

Bean painfully eased out of the saddle and held to the horn for a moment. "That's just what I done," he said. "The buzz saw was named Rick Proctor."

"The kid do this to you?" Klein demanded incredulously.

"He's no kid," Bean said. "He may be only eighteen, but he's the best man I ever tangled with. I don't think I got in one good lick."

Klein shook his head in disgust. "I guess it's a case of me sending a boy to do a man's job instead of the other way around."

"Don't you start in on me," Bean said. "Right now I ain't taking nothing off you or nobody else."

"All right, what happened?"

"I did just what you said," Bean answered. "Then I called his ma a bitch and he hit me. I knew what he'd do, but he was so damned fast I couldn't stop him."

Klein swore softly. What had been meant as a warning to Rick had backfired. The kid had to be taught a lesson. Something permanent.

"I'm gonna kill him," Bean said. "Maybe I'd better do it now instead of later." He paused, dabbing at his nose with his bandanna, then he said, "Joe Hawks is in town."

"The hell he is," Klein said as if he didn't believe it. "How do you know?"

"I got to town too early to wait for Rick, so I went into the hotel bar for a drink. There was Hawks playing poker as big as life."

"You talk to him?"

"No. I figured I'd leave that to you."

"That's right," Klein said. "I'd like to

know why he's here. If he's suspicious, I'd better see him today."

"If he ain't," Bean said, "what's he doing up here? It's a long ride from Kit Carson just for fun."

"He didn't come just for fun." Klein rolled a cigarette and lighted it as he turned this over in his mind, then made his decision. "You get Scott Shell and go back to town after supper. Rick leaves his horse in the livery stable. If he's in the house, send word to him his horse is sick and for him to get down to the stable. If he's out riding, which ain't likely on a night like this, wait for him in the stable. Smoke him down. We should have done it last summer when he was working here while we had the chance."

"It ain't too late," Bean said. "I'll enjoy watching him kick his way into hell."

"Go clean up your face," Klein said. "I'll take care of your horse."

Turning, Bean staggered back to the bunkhouse. Klein watched him until he disappeared inside, unable to understand how it could have happened. Bean was a good barroom brawler who knew every dirty trick in the book. Apparently, Rick Proctor never gave him a chance to use them.

Well, maybe Monte wasn't in shape to shoot straight, but Scott Shell was. He'd take care of Rick, and it had better be quick, too, because if Rick and Hawks ever got together, Rick would kick the roof off.

Funny how two brothers could be so different, he thought. Barney, twenty-five, was mild, good-natured, and easygoing, the kind of man who could be managed. But Rick had been a rebel from the time he was born.

Klein put Bean's horse away, roped and saddled his black gelding, and headed for town. Joe Hawks was a cattle buyer from Kit Carson. He had never to Klein's knowledge been in Proctor City before, and he had never expected the man to come this far north. Most of the cattle he bought came from the area around Kit Carson, so there seemed to be no reason for him to come here.

Klein and several of his men had gathered three small herds off the south range and sold them to Hawks, Klein pretending that the sales were authorized by Jay Proctor. Hawks had accepted everything Klein had said. It was a perfect setup. If his luck held, he could practically clean the range of Rainbow cattle before anyone realized what was happening. By that time, he and his men would be a long way from Rainbow.

Klein railed his black gelding in front of the hotel and swaggered into the lobby. He checked the bar and the dining room, but Hawks was nowhere in sight. Klein walked to the desk, glanced at the register, and saw that Hawks was in Room 10.

"What can I do for you, Curly?" the clerk asked.

"Not a thing," Klein answered. "I just came to see a man."

He wheeled away and climbed the stairs. He found Room 10 and knocked. A man called, "Come in."

He opened the door and stepped inside. Hawks lay sprawled on the bed smoking a cigarette. When he saw who it was, he jumped up and held out his hand. "I thought you'd be coming to see me," he said. "Monte Bean saw me in the bar today, but he left before I had a chance to talk to him."

Klein shook his hand, then closed the door and walked to the window. He turned and stood with his back to it, his thumbs hooked under his belt. He studied Hawks for a moment as he made up his mind what he'd say.

The cattle buyer was middle-aged, a short, slender man who had been in business for twenty years and was well known all over eastern Colorado — too well known to kill unless it became necessary. The only other way to shut him up was to scare him.

"What are you doing in Proctor City?" Klein asked.

"I aimed to ride out and see Jay," Hawks answered, "but I'm tired and decided to wait a day. I just got in this morning. I can tell you one thing from recent experience. Riding a stagecoach all the way from Kit Carson ain't my idea of a pleasure trip."

"You checking up on us?" Klein asked sharply.

"Hell no," Hawks said as if surprised. "I've got a chance to sell some cattle to an outfit near La Junta that wants to fatten a few range steers. I couldn't think of anyone else who would sell this time of year. Since Jay had sold some this winter, I figured he might let a few more go."

"I think you're lying," Klein said. "I think you began wondering if Jay sold them cows or if we rustled them."

"No, I never thought anything of the kind," Hawks said. "I take you for an honest man, Curly. I wouldn't have bought 'em from you if I hadn't thought so."

Klein dropped his hand to his gun butt. "Joe, if you thought we stole them steers, you're dead right. We did. Jay don't know nothing about 'em. We stuck the dinero in our pockets and we aim to sell you some more."

"Oh, I wish you hadn't told me that," Hawks said as if he were shocked. "I can't take any more from you if that's the case. I — I reckon Jay could have me arrested for what I've done already."

"That's right," Klein said. "Now I'll tell you something else. If you open your mouth to anybody — I'll kill you. I may not hear about it right away, but when I do, you're a dead man. Savvy?"

"I savvy, all right," Hawks said, "but why should I tell anybody? I'm in this as deep as you are. Besides, I need more cattle like I was telling you."

"That's smart," Klein said, "but I dunno how far I can trust you no matter how you talk. It would be safer if I rubbed you out right now."

Hawks never carried a gun. Now he shook his head at Klein. "I'm not armed. It would be murder any way you look at it, and I don't think they'd look on murder with favor in Proctor City, even by the Rainbow foreman. You'd be better off to trust me."

Klein had drawn his gun and eared back the hammer. He had expected Hawks to cave in and beg for his life, but the little cattle buyer had not shown the slightest sign

25

of fear. He eased the hammer down and holstered his gun.

"All right, I'll play it your way, Hawks," Klein said. "But get this straight. You catch that stage in the morning and head back for Kit Carson."

"I'll do that, Curly," Hawks said. "I aimed to do that all the time."

"Stay away from Rainbow, too," Klein said. "You'd just make Jay unhappy. I don't think he'd believe you, though. He believes what I tell him."

"I'll bet he does," Hawks said. "Yes sir, I'll bet he does."

Klein walked out and shut the door with a bang. He wasn't at all sure he'd scared Hawks, but he was sure about one thing. He couldn't kill Hawks in the hotel, and the cattleman wasn't likely to leave his room for anything except his meals.

The best thing to do was to let it ride. Chances were Hawks would be greedy enough to buy the next bunch of cattle Klein brought him. It had always been Klein's observation that greed dictated a man's actions more than anything else.

Mounting, Klein left town. The wind was as sharp as ever, and the sky looked more ominous than when he had ridden in a short time ago. Snow would be falling before morning, he told himself, and that would put a crimp in any more cattle stealing for a while.

The thought occurred to him that he'd be smart to leave Rainbow now, while he was ahead of the game. But then he decided against it. He had never been a man to pull out of a game when he was winning and the other fellow still had some money to lose. Right now he was winning, and there were plenty of Rainbow steers to steal from the south range. He'd hang and rattle for a while.

CHAPTER 3

Barney Proctor was on his way to the bunkhouse when his mother called. Turning, he saw her standing on the porch motioning for him to come to her. He hesitated, knowing exactly what this meant. His father wanted to send him on some kind of errand, and this was one night he didn't feel like going anywhere.

He leaned into the wind and headed toward his mother. He had worked too long and too hard to stay in his father's good graces to jump the track now. That had been Rick's way, to say to hell with it and walk out. Sometimes Barney wished he had the guts to do the same thing, but he didn't. He always obeyed, thinking that his loyalty to his father would make him his heir. There was just one thing wrong with his thinking, and he knew what it was: Jay Proctor was crippled, but he might live to be one hundred years old.

When he reached the porch, his mother said, "Pa wants to see you."

"Get inside before you start to chill, ma," Barney said. "That wind is a booger."

She whirled and ran back into the house. Barney followed, shutting the door behind him. His mother stood huddled over the cook stove, her hands extended.

"You've got to stay out of that wind, ma," Barney said sharply. "It'll put you in bed if you ain't careful."

"I know," she said, "but pa decided after supper he had to see you. There was nothing to do but go get you. I had just started when I saw you."

Barney stared at his mother, so thin that a wind like this could blow her away, he told himself. That was his father for you. He didn't give a damn about anybody else's health or well-being, but if you didn't take care of *his* every whim he made life hell for you.

His mother was right, too, about doing what his father asked, Barney knew. She had to live in the same house with him. Barney crossed the kitchen and front room to where Jay sat in his wheelchair beside the window.

"What do you want, pa?" Barney asked.

Startled, Jay turned to look at Barney. "I didn't hear you come in. I was sitting here

29

thinking about that goddamn Milt Smith. I'm gonna kill him, Barney. You hear me? I'm gonna kill him."

Barney knew that his father would order someone else to kill Milt, because Jay hadn't been off Rainbow since his accident a year ago. Barney also knew that if Jay told *him* to shoot Milt Smith, he'd walk out just the way Rick had. Rainbow wasn't worth hanging for. Besides, Barney liked Milt Smith. Everybody did but Jay.

Jay had once been a big, strong man, but now his legs were worthless, shriveled, and too weak to support his body even if he could have moved them. He was ashamed of his legs and kept them covered with a blanket. He ate well, and as far as Barney knew, his father's general health was excellent. He could very well live to be a hundred.

"You'll remember I had Judge Callahan out here the other day," Jay said, "and changed my will again. I'll tell you about it in the morning. What I want you to do now is to ride into town and tell the judge I want to see him tonight. He should have the will drawn up before this, so tell him to bring it and I'll sign it."

Barney hesitated, looking down at his father. This, again, was exactly like Jay

Proctor. It made no difference to him that the wind was kicking up a storm or that it was cold enough to freeze the balls off a brass monkey. Judge Callahan was seventy years old and a ride from town and back might be more than he could manage.

Barney made a point never to argue with his father, but this time he couldn't help it. "It's a bad night to be out, pa. The judge is an old man. He might not want to do it."

"Then tell him he ain't the only lawyer around," Jay snapped. "If he don't want Rainbow business, maybe some younger lawyer will."

Then Jay permitted himself one of his few smiles. "You'll like this will, Barney. I never saw any sense in the story of the Prodigal Son. Hell, he should have stayed where he was and kept right on eating with the hogs. The other son stayed home and took care of everything. *He* was the one who should have had the fatted calf." Jay waggled a forefinger at Barney. "We'll butcher the fatted calf for you. You're the good son who stayed home and took care of everything."

"Yes, pa," Barney said.

He turned and strode back through the kitchen and went outside, not saying anything to his mother. He couldn't help wondering why, if he had stayed home and

31

taken care of everything so well, his father hadn't made him foreman? At least a bastard like Curly Klein wouldn't be running the outfit. But Jay Proctor trusted Klein, and it would take an act of God to change Jay's mind on anything.

While he was saddling his bay gelding Klein walked up to him and said, "It's a bad night for riding, Barney."

"Ain't my idea," Barney said sourly. "Someday I'm gonna tell the old man to stuff it and then I'll ride out of here."

"You ought to do that," Klein agreed blandly. "He don't even pay you top-hand wages, does he?"

"No," Barney said. He stepped into the saddle and took the road to town.

He had trouble finding Callahan. The judge wasn't at his house, and Mrs. Callahan said she thought he was at Doc Doan's place playing poker. If he wasn't, he'd be at Sheriff Osmand's house, or Jeff Houston's. Houston owned the hardware store and was the fourth poker player in the group. All that Mrs. Callahan was sure of was that Judge Callahan was somewhere else playing poker.

"He goes every Thursday no matter how I feel or what I want to do that night," Mrs. Callahan said bitterly. "He'd go even if the house was burning down."

Barney finally found Callahan in Houston's house. When Callahan came to the door, Barney said, "Pa told me to tell you to come out to Rainbow tonight and bring the will. He wants to sign it."

"Tonight? With a storm coming in?" Callahan made no effort to hide his disbelief. "Does he expect to die before morning?"

"He didn't say as to that," Barney answered. "I'm just giving you his message. He says that if you're too old to make the ride tonight, there's plenty of young lawyers who would like to have the Rainbow business."

Callahan was a tall, skinny man who was not as frail as he looked. Still, he was seventy years old and appeared his age with his long white hair and white, goatlike beard. Barney had never liked him, considering him sly and underhanded, although Jay trusted him and took his advice more often than not on legal matters.

Now he stood motionless, still glaring at Barney as if he held him responsible for Jay's request. Then he said coldly, "All right, the king has spoken."

Barney wheeled and strode back to his horse without another word. He had hoped Callahan would say to hell with it. In that case Jay would have to turn to one of the younger lawyers. But Callahan was too shrewd to give up the lucrative Rainbow business.

Mounting, Barney rode to Main Street, hating the prospect of riding home against the biting wind. He contemplated getting a room in the hotel and decided to settle for a drink instead. As he stepped into the bar he noticed that Monte Bean and Scott Shell were hunched over a table in the back of the long room. He did not indicate he had seen them. They were two of the six men Klein had hired since he had been named foreman. They were a clannish lot, and although Barney had no trouble with them, he wasn't friendly with them either.

He stopped at the bar and ordered a drink, wondering how Bean had got his face chewed up. He'd taken some hooraying at supper about it, but had given no explanation.

Barney was still waiting for his drink when a man rose from a table in the back and walked along the bar. He stopped two feet from Barney and threw a coin on the cherrywood. He said in a low tone as if talking to the barkeep, "I want to see you, Barney. Room ten."

The man walked on. Barney hadn't looked

at his face because it was evident that he didn't want anyone to know that he had spoken to Barney. After the man moved on to the lobby door, Barney glanced at his back and thought he recognized Joe Hawks.

Barney reached for his drink and turned the glass thoughtfully with the tips of his fingers, deciding it couldn't be Joe because Hawks never came to Proctor City for business — he usually waited for business to come to him.

Barney took his time, enjoying the warmth of the room. He exchanged a few words with the bartender, then gulped his drink and paid for it, saying, "Gonna be a cold ride home."

The barkeep nodded agreement. "Sure will. Better stay in town."

"I thought of it," Barney admitted, "but I've got to mosey along."

He left the bar, and as soon as he turned the corner in the lobby and was out of sight of anyone in the bar, he ran to the stairs and took them two at a time. He found Room 10, knocked on the door, and was astonished when he saw that it was Joe Hawks who opened the door.

Barney stepped into the room quickly. Hawks shook his hand, saying, "I'm sure glad you showed up in the bar. I wanted to see you, but I was afraid to ride out to Rainbow. Barney, you're looking at a mighty scared man."

Barney believed him. His face was white. He was so nervous his hands were trembling and he couldn't sit down. He motioned for Barney to sit in the one chair in the room and started pacing back and forth.

"What brought you up here?" Barney asked.

"I'll tell you after you answer a question," Hawks said. "Did you know that Curly Klein sold three bunches of Rainbow cattle to me during the past winter, claiming that he was authorized by your father to sell them?"

"Hell no," Barney said, shocked by the remark. "Pa never authorized anyone to sell a single steer."

"That's what Klein did," Hawks said. "Looking back on it, I can see I was damned stupid. I should have waited until I had a chance to talk to you, but I knew Klein was your foreman and I knew your pa trusted him, so I thought it was legitimate."

"Sure you would," Barney said.

"Well, after we settled up the last time, Klein said he'd have more to sell, that your pa was cleaning off the south range and was going to stock it with pure-bred shorthorns.

I got to thinking about it afterward and it struck me that Jay wouldn't be doing anything of the kind. He had good stock and I even remembered him saying one time that he'd get along with what he had, that in the long run you didn't make anything by buying expensive bulls. I got suspicious and figured maybe I'd been buying stolen cattle. I could see a cell waiting for me in Canon City."

"We wouldn't press charges against you," Barney said. "I guess this proves what some of us have been thinking about Klein. But pa still trusts him. I don't think he'll believe me when I tell him."

"That's what I was afraid of," Hawks said. "I aimed to get a horse from the livery stable and ride out to Rainbow, but that damned stage ride from Kit Carson crippled me up. Besides, Klein changed my mind about going out to Rainbow. He showed up late this afternoon. Monte Bean had seen me in the bar a little before that. Klein guessed why I was here. He told me to get on the stage in the morning and if I said a word to anybody about the stolen cattle, he'd kill me. He pulled his gun and acted like he might shoot me right here in my room."

"He was bluffing," Barney said.

37

"About shooting me here in the room," Hawks agreed, "but not about the rest. He's a killer. I'd bet my last nickel on it. What should we do?"

Barney rose. "You go ahead and take the stage. If you ain't around here, he probably won't bother you. I'll tell pa in the morning, but I know what he'll say. He'll probably accuse me of lying just to give Klein a bad name."

"I've got plenty of proof in my office in Kit Carson," Hawks said.

"As soon as the weather clears, I'll get hold of Rick and we'll take a sashay down to the south range. We'll probably go on to Kit Carson and look at your records. When I get back, I'll report to the sheriff, though I ain't sure he'll do anything."

"You can count on me being on that stage," Hawks said. "I wish I hadn't come. A letter would have been enough. I hope Bean and Shell didn't see me talking to you. If they did, I won't live long enough to get on the stage."

Barney shook hands with Hawks and left the room. He wanted another drink, but he couldn't risk letting Bean or Shell know he hadn't left when he'd walked out of the bar. He mounted and rode home, a sick feeling of frustration possessing him.

Sure, he, Barney Proctor, good-natured and easygoing, had been the obedient son who had stayed home and taken care of things. But the bitter truth was that when it came to a showdown, Jay Proctor would believe Curly Klein before he would believe his own son.

CHAPTER 4

Rick stared at the right triangle he had drawn on a sheet of scratch paper. It lay on the desk in front of him, but he wasn't seeing it. He'd come to his room right after supper to do tomorrow's assignment and that was as far as he had gone. All he could think of was his mother's letter that Mrs. Laird had handed to him when he'd finished eating.

"I got this out of the post office today," Mrs. Laird said, "but in all the excitement I clean forgot about it."

Now he picked it up and read it again.

Wednesday afternoon

Dear Rick,

I've written to the sheriff about your father and today I'm writing to Dr. Doan. Maybe none of you can do anything, but somebody has to. I know your father better than anyone else. All week he's been a seething volcano. He's ready to erupt.

I know you hate to come home, but I think you'd better come Friday right after school. Perhaps it won't do any good to tell him you're going to marry Milt Smith's daughter, but I think you ought to. Maybe there's nothing anybody can do, but we've got to try.

With all my love,
Mom

Rick slipped the letter back into the envelope and laid it on the desk. No, it wouldn't do any good to tell his father he was marrying Ruth Smith. That might only make the situation worse. Maybe he could talk his mother into leaving Rainbow when he was home. He'd tried before and failed, but the situation must be getting worse or his mother would not have written at all.

With so much on his mind, he felt as if he were a hundred years old instead of only eighteen. He sat another five minutes tapping his pencil against the edge of his desk, and then, because he couldn't just sit there any longer, he decided to ride out to Milt Smith's Rafter S. The least he could do was to warn Milt.

Rick blew out the lamp and left his room. He tip-toed along the hall to the front door, hoping he wouldn't waken Mrs. Laird. He took his hat and sheepskin off the rack near the front door, put them on, and stepped outside. A cold fierce wind whipped at his face and made his eyes water. The snow would be here soon, he thought.

When he reached the livery stable, the night man, Larry Simms, asked, "You ain't riding out tonight, are you, Rick?"

"Thought I would," Rick said.

He saddled his sorrel gelding and rode out through the archway into the street, Simms muttering that it must be wonderful to be young and full of vinegar.

Rick took the road that led to Milt Smith's Rafter S. The road forked east of the long bridge that spanned the Big Sandy, one fork turning upstream to the Rafter S and the other following the bridge and going on to Rainbow and then into the sand hills beyond.

Rick thought about Milt as he rode. Milt was not a hating man, although he had plenty of reason to hate Jay Proctor, who had harassed him in a dozen ways for more than a year. But he was as stubborn and determined as Jay was, especially when it came to his land.

He finally reached the Smith house and tied his sorrel, then called to announce his presence.

The door opened a crack and Ruth shouted, "Who is it?"

"Rick."

"Well, for goodness sakes, come in before you freeze to death," she cried. "I didn't expect you tonight."

Rick stepped up on the porch and into the room. Ruth closed the door quickly behind him.

"You haven't kissed me since Sunday night and this is Thursday," she said. "Do your duty."

He laughed and kissed her, and said, "The most pleasant duty a man ever had."

"And don't you forget it after we're married," she said.

Milt stood in front of the fireplace watching them with amusement. "Well now, Rick," he said, "after you get done with that lallygagging, maybe Ruth can fix you some hot coffee to warm you up. What brings you out on a night like this? I don't think you'd come on a school night just to kiss Ruth."

"Now what better reason would bring him on this or any night?" Ruth demanded hotly.

Milt raised both hands in mock surrender. "All right, all right, it's a good reason. I just figured that maybe there was something more."

"There is," Rick said.

He looked at Milt and swallowed, not knowing how to say what he had to say. Now that he was here, it seemed presumptuous for anyone his age to give advice to a man like Milt Smith.

The older man was a head shorter than Rick, stocky, with a square face and a wide, out-thrusting jaw that hinted at his stubborn nature. He was, Rick knew, absolutely incapable of backing down when anyone pushed him. That was where Jay Proctor had made his mistake. The bulldozing tactics that had worked with other ranchers in the valley had not worked with Milt Smith.

Ruth, glancing at Rick and then at her father, sensed the sudden tension, and said, "I'll get you a cup of coffee, Rick."

After she disappeared into the kitchen, Milt said, "You're the most man of any eighteen-year-old I ever seen, so I'm not going to discount anything you say. Go ahead."

Rick swallowed and stared at the floor. He knew that Milt had not approved of his and Ruth's engagement, thinking they were too young, but he hadn't fought it, either. He'd said the same thing before, that Rick was no ordinary, hell-raising teen-age boy.

"I guess that bucking pa like I have since I was a little shaver made me grow up faster'n most kids," Rick said. "He was ornery and mean before his accident, but he's worse now."

"Is he sane?" Milt asked.

"I don't think so," Rick said, "but I don't know how you go at proving a man's crazy. If we went to court, I doubt that Barney would testify that pa was crazy. Klein and his crew sure wouldn't. That would just leave ma and me, and I ain't been home enough this year to know how he is."

"Klein makes it worse," Milt said bitterly. "I think he keeps Jay worked up against me, though Jay hated me before Klein started rodding Rainbow. He blames me for his accident, but I don't see how he can. He rode over here to make me an offer for the Rafter S and my dog ran out and barked. That boogered Jay's horse and it threw him against the end of the horse trough. Hell, how can a sane man say that was my fault?"

"A sane man wouldn't, Milt," Rick said. "But you know pa. You're either for him or against him. There's nothing in between. I don't even exist as far as he's concerned."

"There was a time when we were neighbors and worked together on a lot of things," Milt said, "but we haven't done that for a long time. Not since he started buying his neighbors out. We could still be neighbors if he wanted it that way."

"It ain't so much that you're to blame for his accident," Rick said. "He uses that for an excuse. What really gets him is that he's bluffed everybody else into selling except you. He won't stop pushing at you as long as you're alive, Milt. I had a letter from ma today. She sent one to Doc Doan, too. That's why I rode out. She says he's like a seething volcano, ready to erupt."

Ruth had brought the coffee and Milt and Rick were silent for a moment. Rick moved to stand at one end of the fireplace and remained there sipping his coffee as Milt lit his pipe. For a moment there was no sound in the room except the heavy breathing of the two men and the snapping of the wood in the fireplace.

Finally Ruth said, "I heard what you said about Jay, Rick. Hasn't he always been a seething volcano?"

"Let's say he's been a smoldering one." Rick looked directly at Milt. "Ma says he's ready to order your murder."

Milt shrugged. "I ain't surprised. Don't worry about me, Rick. My grandfather built this house as strong as a fort for protection against the Cheyennes and Arapahoes. It's still solid with shutters for the windows and bars for the doors. I keep a full barrel of water in the kitchen and plenty of grub and ammunition. We can hold out for a long time."

"It's Ruth I'm worried about," Rick said. "Send her away."

Milt stared blankly at Rick as if he couldn't believe what he'd heard. "She's as good a shot as any man. Why should I send her away?"

Rick held his tongue for a moment as he fought his temper, but he couldn't hold it. He said with cold fury, "Because she's a woman and I love her and I want to marry her, and by God, I don't want her killed in a crazy range war that shouldn't happen."

Milt's face turned red and he began to swell up like an aroused turkey gobbler.

"Now just hold on, you two," Ruth said sharply. "I love both of you and I don't want you getting into a ruckus over me. Of course, I'll stay here, Rick. It's where I belong. Where else would I go?"

"Mrs. Laird has an extra bedroom," Rick said. "She'd put you up until the row's over."

"Just when will that be?" Milt demanded.

"It'll be over when one of two things happen," Rick said. "When pa dies or when you sell out."

"Either one's gonna be a long time coming," Milt shot back. "Jay's healthy enough and you know I ain't gonna sell. If you rode out here to ask me to sell to Jay, you had a cold ride for nothing."

"No, I rode out here to warn you," Rick said, "but that's got nothing to do with Ruth."

"I know, I know," Milt said, the hostility going out of him. "She's a woman and I've always acted like she was a boy. I wanted a son so damned bad I could have cried the night she was born, but after her mother died, I decided the good Lord knew what he was doing when he gave me a girl."

He paused and shook his head at Rick. "Well, my friend, I don't want her killed any more than you do, but I've gone over this with her a hundred times because I've seen it coming, knowing Jay as I do, but she won't go. I've asked her to."

"I'm sorry," Rick said. "I should have known that's what she'd say. Some ways she's almost as stubborn as you are, Milt."

"Rick Proctor, I resent that," she said angrily. "If you rode out here to pick a fight —"

"Milt, if I stayed here and helped you fight," Rick said, ignoring Ruth, "would you send her away?"

"I'm the one who decides whether I stay of go," Ruth said. "Nobody's sending me anywhere until I make up —"

Milt held up a hand. "You're dead right about her being almost as stubborn as I am. You know, Rick, if I could have picked out a son, I'd sure have picked you, which is the reason I didn't raise Cain when you two got engaged, but since you ain't my son, I wouldn't ever expect you to fight against your pa and your own outfit."

"It ain't my outfit anymore," Rick said, "and I never picked Jay Proctor for my father. I don't figure I owe him anything." He turned toward the door.

Ruth said contritely, "Don't be mad at me, Rick. I've got to stay here. Don't you see?"

"I reckon I do," he said, "but that don't make me like it."

He kissed her and opened the door and went out into the cold night.

CHAPTER 5

By the time Rick reached town a few flakes of snow were in the air. Several inches would be on the ground by morning, he thought. He wondered whether the storm would force Jay to postpone his move. He decided it wouldn't, that it would take more than a blizzard to persuade Jay Proctor to change his mind on anything.

Main Street was dark except for the hotel lobby and bar, the Silver Streak saloon, and the livery stable. When he approached the archway of the stable, he saw that Larry Simms was standing in the cone of down-thrown light from the lantern hanging above him.

Simms said in a loud tone, "Glad you're back, Rick. A man can freeze to death in this wind."

He moved to one side of the archway and motioned for Rick to stay away from the light. Something was wrong, but Rick didn't know what. He reined up and dismounted as Simms whispered, "A couple of men are waiting to kill you." He reached for the reins, adding, "Say something. Loud."

"I'm glad to get in," Rick said very loudly. "Now I'm gonna get into bed and stay there."

"I'll take care of your horse," Simms said, and led the animal through the archway.

Rick drew his gun and moved to the corner of the stable, finding this hard to believe. No one had ever tried to kill him and he didn't see any reason for anybody to try now, unless Monte Bean had come back to town to get square for the beating he had taken. That didn't make sense, not to Rick anyway.

Simms had barely cleared the archway with Rick's horse when Rick heard boots pounding along the runway. Two men dashed into the street a moment later.

"You looking for me?" Rick called.

They whirled toward him, skidding and kicking up dust. Guns already drawn, they fired as they turned. Both shots were wild. Rick let go at the one nearest to him just as Simms fired a shotgun from inside the stable.

The man Rick shot went down as cleanly as if a rope had jerked his feet out from under him. The second one didn't stay to fight, boogered perhaps by the shotgun blast. He lunged out of the lantern light toward the far corner of the stable. Rick pitched two quick shots at him and missed, then he was out of sight.

"Take a look at this one, Larry," Rick shouted at Simms, who rushed out of the stable, still holding his shotgun.

Rick raced after the fleeing man. He cleared the corner and fired at the sounds of his footsteps and knew at once it was a waste of powder. The narrow lane between the stable and Houston's hardware store was black dark. Rick ran after the man, almost fell over some trash, recovered his footing, and went on. When he reached the rear of the buildings, the man was nowhere in sight and things were deathly quiet.

For a moment Rick stood motionless, listening. A few seconds later he heard the beat of hoofs and then the sound was lost in the wind. Rick holstered his gun and returned to the front of the stable. Simms was standing beside the fallen man.

"He's dead," Simms said. "You couldn't have done no better in the daylight. You hit him right in the brisket."

The deadman was wearing a red bandanna. Rick stooped and jerked it away from his face. It was Scott Shell! Rick straightened and shook his head. He had never had any trouble with Shell. Sure, he was Monte Bean's friend, but so were all the Rainbow men Klein had hired.

"Why would Shell want to kill you?" Simms asked. "He's a Rainbow hand, ain't he?"

"I don't know," Rick said. "Was the other man masked?"

Simms nodded. "Wore a bandanna just like this one did."

"Got any notion who he was?"

Simms shook his head. "No. They came into the stable about half an hour after you got your horse. They wanted to know if your horse was here and I said no, that you'd just left. They asked where you'd gone and I said I didn't know, so then they said they were gonna wait in back and for me to watch and sing out when you showed up."

"How'd you know they were fixing to kill me?"

"I heard scraps of talk from where they were standing between the end of the stable and the corral. One of 'em said something about killing the kid and later on something else about you being more dangerous than Barney. I figured it was plain enough."

"Thanks, Larry," Rick said, "though I

53

don't know how you really thank a man for saving your life. If I'd just ridden in and started taking care of my horse, they'd have gunned me down sure."

"That's what I figured," Simms agreed, "so I thought if you just stayed out of the light and made them come to you, you could take care of yourself. You don't need to thank me at all. I figured I was saving my own hide. I had a hunch they'd come back and beef me after they got you, figuring I might identify 'em."

Men had drifted out of the hotel lobby and bar and Silver Streak saloon. Doc Doan appeared a little later carrying his black bag. The men asked several questions, but only one seemed important once they understood it had been a trap to shoot Rick. Why would a Rainbow cowhand want to kill him?

"I don't know," Rick said. "Damn it, I just don't know. I never had any trouble with Shell and he's been on Rainbow more'n a year."

Doan rose from where he'd been kneeling beside Shell. "You men tote the body over to my place," the doctor said. "Houston, you get a coffin over first thing in the morning."

"Sure," the hardware man said. "I guess the cheapest one I've got will do."

"It'll be too good for a bastard like him," Doan said. "If he's got any friends in the country, I suppose they'd be at Rainbow."

"Klein would be the one to notify," Rick said.

"I'll get word to him in the morning," Doan said. He added in a low tone, "Take care, Rick. Looks like Klein is aiming to put you out of the way."

"Looks that way, all right," Rick agreed. "He sent Monte Bean to town to whip me, but Monte didn't get the job done."

"The hell he did." Doan wheeled to face Simms. "Could the other man have been Bean?"

"Yeah, I guess he could," Simms said. "I didn't see his face, but he was about Bean's size."

"You didn't recognize his voice?" Doan pressed.

Simms shook his head. "I don't see the Rainbow hands very often, so I don't hear their voices. Them new hands Klein hired always leave their horses in the Red Front stable, not here."

"Where's our fat sheriff?" Doan shouted as he looked around the circle of men. "By God, he ought to be here when a man's been killed."

"He's too comfortable sitting around the

fire at home," somebody said.

"I'll go tell him," Rick said.

"Yeah, I reckon you'd better," the doctor said, "but don't let him put you into jail. This is a case of justifiable homicide if I've ever seen one."

"I don't aim to go to jail," Rick said.

As he strode toward Sheriff Osmand's house, he wondered what the lawman would say. There were no lights in the house when Rick yanked on the bell pull. It took several more yanks before a light appeared in the front room.

A moment later the door opened and Osmand said, "What the hell are you getting me out of bed for?" Then he saw who it was, and his tone became less surly. "Oh, it's you, Rick. Come on in before I freeze to death." He saw the snow on Rick's shoulders. "So the storm finally started, eh?"

Rick stepped inside and Osmand shut the door. Rick said, "I shot and killed Scott Shell a few minutes ago. He tried to kill me."

"The hell you did," Osmand said, shocked. "Got any witness that says he tried to kill you?"

"Larry Simms."

"That Shell was a tough hand," Osmand said, "but then most of the Rainbow boys are." He scratched the back of his fat neck.

"Now this don't add up one bit, boy. You're Jay Proctor's son. Shell worked for your dad. Why would he try to kill you?"

"I wish I knew," Rick said, and told Osmand how it happened. He added, "I've got a hunch that Monte Bean was the other man. I think you ought to ride out to Rainbow in the morning and ask a few questions."

"Don't tell me what I ought to do," Osmand muttered. "I sure ain't goin' if the storm gets bad. He wouldn't admit nothin' anyhow. A man like that never does." He peered at Rick a moment, then rubbed a hand across his face. "I ain't gonna arrest you tonight, but you stay in town. Your story don't make sense."

Anger stirred in Rick. "You think I'm lying?"

"I dunno. I'll check it out with Simms tomorrow. It'll wait till morning."

"Reckon so," Rick said, and left the house.

He half expected Osmand to react that way. He'd probably just talk to Simms in the morning and drop it there. Rick's anger faded. At best Osmand was a fat nothing and not worth giving a second thought. His mind turned to Jay Proctor.

The volcano was erupting, all right, but not in the way Rick's mother had expected.

Maybe the shooting tonight and the fight with Bean had nothing to do with Jay and his feud with Milt Smith. In any case, Rick's trouble went back to Curly Klein. He'd go home tomorrow, Rick told himself, and ask some questions. He didn't aim to sit still. Not after he'd been shot at. Maybe he could bring things to a head and get them settled.

CHAPTER 6

Mary Proctor lay on her back, her eyes open, the night blackness surrounding her. She remained motionless, not wanting to make the slightest sound that would waken Jay. She had shared his bed until his accident After that, using the pretext that it would be easier for him to sleep if he had the bed to himself, she had moved to a cot on the other side of the room.

Actually she slept no better than she had before, but perhaps Jay did. At least he had said nothing about wanting her back in his bed. Now she listened to his steady snoring, knowing it was near daylight and that he would soon be yelling at her to get up and build a fire in the kitchen and help him out of bed.

She enjoyed the silence and the peace, and for a while she did not feel the evil that surrounded Jay like a great, angry cloud when he was awake. She had loved him at one time. When they were first married. But as the years went on, Jay had changed. And now, ever since the accident, she hardly knew him. In fact, she hated him, not with the murderous fury which characterized his feeling for Milt Smith, but with a quiet hate that had built slowly over the years, a hate she had never verbalized to anyone. She had never expressed it by word or act, but it was there. Mary guessed she hated Jay enough to kill him. Perhaps someday she would do it.

Suddenly she began to cry softly. Maybe she should have killed him a long time ago. Maybe by letting him live she was to blame for what had happened to Barney and Rick. She wiped her eyes, but the tears still ran down her cheeks as she thought of her boys.

Jay had broken Barney when he was a small boy, and he remained broken to this day. This power that Jay had over Barney was what frightened Mary the most. Sometime — and she thought it would be soon — Jay would give Barney the order to kill Milt Smith, and she was afraid he would do it. She often wondered if he had a mind of his own or if Jay had hypnotized him.

The difference in the disposition of the two boys had been evident almost from the day they were born. Barney had wanted to be cuddled, he had sought approval as soon as he was big enough to understand that some acts brought a smile and a kiss and other acts produced a scolding or a spanking.

Rick had been a maverick from the first. He hadn't seemed to care whether he received a smile or a scolding. Jay had never broken him and he never would. She wished she hadn't asked Rick to come home Friday after school, but maybe he wouldn't come. Even if he did, he wouldn't stay.

She could understand and submit to the various ways Jay had of dominating her. She had known he was that way before she married him. Maybe that was what she really wanted from a husband, but it was not what she wanted for her sons. That, she knew, was the real reason she hated Jay.

Sometimes she wondered if she had a talent for seeing the future. She knew that sooner or later Jay would order Barney to do something that would be his undoing, and sooner or later he would do something equally stupid that would widen the gap between him and Rick so that it could never be bridged and Rick would go away forever.

She saw very little of Rick now, only when she went to Proctor City on Saturdays to shop and had time to stop at Mrs. Laird's.

She worried about Rick even though she knew he could take care of himself. But never getting to see her son was painful, and the more pain she felt, the more she hated Jay Proctor.

Daylight was beginning to creep into the room through the east windows. The end of the peace and quiet was at hand. She would start another endless day of waiting on Jay, a day of listening to him yell orders at her, which she would obey with never a word of thanks or appreciation from him.

A few minutes later she heard him snore louder than usual. Apparently it woke him, for after a few seconds he bellowed, "Get up, Mary, and build the fire and get me out of the damned bed."

She didn't move and she didn't answer. She pretended she hadn't heard. It would be wonderful to lie here, to disobey Jay for once. He couldn't do anything to her except whip her with his tongue.

When she gave no sign of getting up, he bellowed, "Damn it, woman, get up. You heard me."

There was no reason under the sun why she should get up now. She had nothing pressing to do, and time would hang heavily on her hands before the day was out, but old habits were too strong. He would keep yelling until she got up.

She rose, pulled on her slippers and a robe, and went into the kitchen. She built a fire in the cook stove, put the teakettle on the front of the stove, poured water into the coffeepot, dribbled ground coffee into the pot, and set it beside the teakettle. With these chores attended to, she built a fire in the heater in the front room.

When she returned to the bedroom, she slipped out of her nightgown, and dressed. Usually she took care of Jay first, and now he reminded her loudly that he wanted to get out of bed and into his wheelchair. She ignored him, as much of a declaration of independence as she had ever made.

He was furious with her when she finally rolled his chair to the side of the bed and helped him move into it. The upper part of his body was as strong as ever, and he had learned to use his arms to help lift himself into his chair.

She wheeled him into the kitchen, poured hot water, into a basin, and set it on a small stand beside his chair. She brought his shaving gear and a towel and laid them beside the pan of water, then lighted a bracket lamp beside the window.

Shaving was one of the few things he could do entirely by himself, and he took great pride in it. She set about getting breakfast, wondering how long he could survive. Not physically, for he was healthy enough that the doctor said he might live to a ripe old age. Rather, she wondered how long his mind could hold out.

Jay had always been a man who drove himself, to prove he was superior to other men. He could work harder than anyone else in order to satisfy his life's ambition: to possess more wealth than any other cowman in the county.

How could a man like that go on being as dependent on others as Jay was? She didn't think he could last much longer, and she suspected the fall had unbalanced him. His hatred for Milt Smith had reached the point where it had become ridiculous. There was simply no logical reason for it, and no sane man would feel the way he did.

By the time he finished shaving, his breakfast was ready. He wheeled himself to the table as she set his plate of bacon and flapjacks in front of him and poured his coffee. He asked, "Ain't you going to eat?"

She wasn't sure that she could, but she didn't feel like arguing, so she said, "Of course." She poured coffee for herself, forked the last of the flapjacks onto her plate and brought it to the table. She sat down, but she ate very little. At least she went through the motions of eating and that satisfied him.

When he finished, he said, "Roll me into the front room."

She obeyed. Full daylight had come now, but the light was still thin. As she stood at a window and looked out upon the wide channel of the Big Sandy, she saw that it was snowing. She guessed that two or three inches had fallen, and the snow was still coming down very hard in big flakes. Visibility was cut down so she could not even see the other side of the Big Sandy. Jay, of course, could not see Milt Smith's house.

He filled and lighted his pipe, then sat staring at the snow. He did not even pick up his glasses. She wondered how he could sit there all day, but he would, leaving the window only for his meals.

"Get on with your work, woman," he said. "I'm all right."

Of course he was, she thought, glancing down at his strong face, the sharp nose, the dominating chin. Yes, he was all right, but it never occurred to him that she might not be all right.

Nothing, she thought bitterly, as she turned away from the window, ever occurred to him that did not center upon himself. She went into the bedroom and made his bed, then she opened her bureau drawer and took out a small revolver.

She had not fired the gun for years, but there had been a time when she had done some target shooting with Jay. She had finally beaten him one Sunday afternoon. That was the last time they ever shot together. He called it an accident that she had beaten him, but she often told herself that he had never given her another chance to repeat the "accident."

She told herself that if she took the gun and went into the front room and placed the muzzle to the back of Jay's head and fired, she would save Milt Smith's life and maybe save her boys, too. At least Barney would be his own man, and Rick could come back to Rainbow and stay.

She couldn't do it. She knew that it would take something terrible to force her to kill him. She couldn't imagine what it would be. She only knew it would come. She replaced the gun in the bureau drawer, made her bed, and left the bedroom.

As she crossed the front room, she saw that Jay had picked up his .45 from the stand where he kept it beside his glasses and pipe and tobacco. He was holding the big revolver on his lap and staring at it. He did not glance at her as she walked past, but she knew what was in his mind. He was daydreaming about using the gun to kill Milt Smith, but what would he do when he came out of his daydream and faced the reality of being a prisoner in a wheelchair?

As she washed the dishes, she had a chilling sensation of knowing what was going to happen. He would send for Barney. He often said that Barney was his feet. If he could not kill Milt Smith himself, he would send Barney to do it.

She had finished washing and drying the dishes when Jay yelled, "Mary, come in here."

She walked into the front room, breathing hard, and when he said, "Go out and find Barney, and tell him I want to see him," she felt her stomach muscles tie up into knots. This was exactly what she had known she would hear.

She stood motionless, staring down at him, a strong feeling of rebellion in her. Maybe this was the time to tell him she would not do what he ordered. Then she knew she would. She would only make her life harder if she disobeyed. He would find some way to summon Barney whether she did it or not.

"What do you want with Barney?" she asked.

This surprised him and brought his glance to her face. She had never questioned him before about why he told her to do something. He scowled, then he said testily, "What the hell difference does it make to you?"

"He's my son, too," she said.

He laughed, a very unpleasant sound. "Yeah, I guess he is your son, too. But he takes my orders, not yours. Now go get him."

Turning, she trudged back into the kitchen. She pulled her boots on, then slipped into her coat and tugged the wool cap down over her ears. She went out through the back door and crossed the yard, noticing that the snow was four or five inches deep and still coming down hard.

She glanced at the bunkhouse, hesitated, then went on to the barn. She stepped into the stable and saw that several men were standing in the runway talking. One was the foreman, Curly Klein. He frowned when he saw her, then walked to where she stood just inside the door.

"What can I do for you, Miz Proctor?" he asked.

He was a burly, rough-featured man, as

tall as Rick and heavier of bone and muscle. In time, she thought, Rick would be as big. Actually she was afraid of Klein, but he was the kind of man who appealed to Jay. As long as Jay was in command, Curly Klein would continue to ramrod Rainbow.

"I came out to tell Barney that his father wants to see him," she said.

"He's back yonder," Klein said, jerking a hand at one of the back stalls. "I'll tell him."

She nodded, hesitated, and then said, "I want him to come in through the kitchen. He'll have snow on his boots and I don't want him tracking up the front room."

Turning, she plodded back through the snow, her head down. The air was very cold and the wind that whipped the snowflakes past her made the air seem colder than it was. She was getting old, she thought, for the cold seemed to bite into her more than usual.

She was only forty-five, but she felt much older, and she knew she looked it. It was the hard work that had done it to her, one more mark she had against Jay. She had asked several times for Jay to hire a girl to help her around the house, but he always dismissed her request as if it were foolish.

"You ain't big, but you're strong," Jay would say. "You can be your own hired girl."

She went into the kitchen, pulled off her boots and left them on the porch beside the back door, then took off her cap and coat. Shivering, she held her hands out over the stove. If they were poor as they had been twenty-six years ago when they were married it would be different, but they weren't poor anymore. They could afford help in the house.

She was still standing there, her thoughts running bitter and hostile, when Barney came in, kicking snow off his boots and slapping his Stetson against his legs.

"So you don't want me tracking up the front-room floor," he said. "When did you get so particular?"

"Just this morning," she said.

She looked up at him, thinking that his round, pleasant face was not at all like Jay's or Rick's. He was simply too good-natured for his own good. Suddenly she reached out and gripped his arms. He was surprised and tried to back away, for she was not one to make any gesture of affection and it embarrassed him.

"Barney," she whispered, "don't do what he's going to ask you to do. I've got a feeling about this, a different feeling than last night when he sent for you."

He blinked, then nodded and grinned.

"Sure, ma, sure," he said.

She dropped her hands to her sides and watched as he crossed to the front room, his boots leaving wet spots on the kitchen floor.

CHAPTER 7

Barney had no idea what Jay wanted with him beyond telling him about the will. He wondered how his mother knew. Jay was not likely to have told her. He never told her anything. That was one part of their life which had not changed over the years. His mother ran the house, and Jay ran everything else.

Whatever Jay had thought up for him to do must be something terrible. His mother had never before tried to tell him anything or keep him from doing anything. Not since he had been a small boy anyhow.

It was so unusual that he stopped halfway across the room to stare at the back of his father's head. Suddenly he was uneasy, for he was remembering that he had something to tell Jay, and he was afraid to say it. For a moment he had forgotten all about Joe Hawks.

"Where the hell are you?" Jay said irritably. "Get over here where I can see you."

Barney moved on to stand beside Jay, who tipped his head back to look up at his son. He asked, "What happened to you? I heard you talking to ma and after that you came on into the room and then you stopped. Get a cramp in your gitalong?"

"No, I stopped to think awhile." Barney rubbed his chin. "Pa, I've got something to tell you. You ain't gonna want to hear it."

Jay scowled. "Damn it, you're my son and heir. If you've got something to say, go ahead and say it."

"I figured you wouldn't believe me."

Jay threw up his hands. "My God, I never knew you to lie to me. Why would I think you were starting now?"

"No, I never have lied to you, pa." Barney's heart was pounding. Now that he'd started he couldn't back out. "It's just that you trust Curly."

"You bet I trust Curly. He's the best ramrod I ever had. Maybe it's because he's the first one I've had who sees things the way I do. He's tough and I like that." He stopped, his lips tightening against his teeth. "Are you trying to say I shouldn't trust Curly?"

"That's exactly what I'm saying," Barney said. "He's stealing us blind."

73

Jay blinked and rubbed a hand across his face. "I guess I ain't hearing good today. If you said Curly's stealing us blind, which is what I thought you said, then you're right, I don't believe it. If you'd said he'd raped a woman or shot a man, I'd believe you, but stealing . . ." He shook his head. "No, that's too much for me."

"All right," Barney said. "I told Joe Hawks you wouldn't believe me. What did you want to see me about?"

"What about Hawks?" Jay demanded. "Go ahead and tell me what you know."

"I went into the hotel bar last night and Joe Hawks was there. He told me to come up to his room. Would you believe what he told me?"

"Reckon I would," Jay said. "I've done business with him long enough to know he's honest."

"He told me he'd bought three small herds of Rainbow cattle from Curly this winter. He knew you were laid up, so he figured Curly had authority to sell."

"I'll be damned." Jay gripped the arms of his chair, his gaze pinned on Barney's face. "Did you believe him? I mean, did he sound like he was telling the truth?"

"He sure did," Barney answered. "He was scared, figuring he'd been buying stolen cattle. I guess he could see himself getting sent to the Canon City pen, but I told him you wouldn't hold him responsible. He had a right to figure that Curly was acting under your orders."

"Yeah, by God, he had a right to," Jay said. "I guess everybody in the country knows how much I think of Curly and how much I trust him."

He turned his head to stare thoughtfully at the falling snow, then he said, "Callahan brought the will out last night. I said I'd tell you about it this morning. You're the sole heir to Rainbow. Your ma and brother get nothing, but I did put in another clause saying that if you weren't alive at the time of my death, Curly would inherit the spread." He paused and scratched his nose. "Now I dunno. Maybe you'd better go into town and tell the sheriff I want to see him."

"I'll go into town Monday," Barney said. "This ain't the kind of weather town dudes like to be out riding."

"Reckon not," Jay said. "There's no hurry about seeing Osmand, but you're gonna be out in this weather. I've waited on Milt Smith all I'm going to. I want you to tell him that. He's got twenty-four hours to sell out to me."

So this was what his mother was worried

about, Barney thought. He guessed he had known all the time. He had simply refused to think about Milt Smith, hoping that Jay would get over his hate and knowing all the time he wouldn't. Staring at his father, it seemed to Barney that Jay Proctor had suddenly become a different man. Up to now, he had been perfectly rational.

Barney remembered a bad horse they'd had a year or so ago. Nobody would ride him, so they'd finally sold him. That animal had been an outlaw and he had showed it in his eyes. Barney had never seen another horse with that crazy, wild look, and now it seemed to him that his father had the same expression.

"Milt's a stubborn man," Barney said. "I don't think he'll bluff."

"I ain't bluffing," Jay screamed, his face turning red. He picked up his revolver and waved it around his head. "Don't let him think I'm bluffing. Tell him he ain't stalling me no longer. By God, I want his ranch and I'm gonna have it."

"His family's been on that place a long time," Barney said. "He won't leave as long as he's alive."

"Then we'll kill him." Jay glared at Barney. "Tell him that. Be sure he understands it."

"We'll kill him?" Barney took a long breath. "You don't know what you're saying, pa. That's murder."

"Don't tell me I don't know what I'm saying," Jay raged. "Call it murder if you want to. I call it an execution, but whatever you call it, Milt Smith's gonna wind up dead if he don't sell to me. Now you tell him that."

"Pa, you can't do it," Barney said. "There's some law in this country. Maybe it ain't much, but it's enough that it won't stand for murder."

"The law in this country is Proctor law and it'll stand for whatever I tell it to." Jay's face turned redder than ever until it was almost purple. He added in a low voice, "You're arguing with me, son. You've never done that before. I don't like it. I can still change my will any way I want to. Now are you gonna go see Milt or not?"

Barney hadn't known until that moment that he had been arguing, but now he realized he was doing exactly what Rick had done so many times and what he had promised himself he would never do. In that instant he could see himself losing everything that he had gained by his patience, but suddenly it didn't seem very important.

Still, old habit prevailed, and he said, "Yes, pa. I'll go see him right away."

"Good," Jay said, pleased. "Let me know what he says when you get back. He always used to be reasonable. I don't think he'll give us any trouble."

Barney wheeled and strode across the living room and into the kitchen. Jay said "we" and "us" as if he would be the one leading the crew across the Big Sandy to kill Milt, but he'd be sitting right there by the window as he always was these days. Barney and Curley Klein and Monte Bean and the rest of the crew would do the killing, and they'd do the hanging.

Barney went on out through the back door, icy wind hitting him the instant he stepped off the porch. His mother had gone out to get a bucket of coal.

She hurried back toward the house when she saw Barney, calling to him, "What did he want?"

"You acted like you knew," Barney said.

"I was guessing," his mother said.

"He ordered me to tell Milt Smith he's got twenty-four hours to sell out," Barney said. "If he don't, we're going to kill him."

"We?" Mary said, so softly that Barney barely heard.

"Yeah, we," Barney said. "You've been trying to tell me he'd gone loco, but I didn't believe it. I believe it now. He talked like killing Milt Smith was no different than going after a coyote. He's crazy as a loon."

"Oh, Barney," Mary said, "I'm glad to hear you say that. I've known it for months. He started getting that way after his accident. I guess he just brooded so long that he went batty. What are we going to do?"

"I don't know, but I've got a hunch that Curly will do anything pa says." Barney slapped his hands together and stomped his feet. "I'll go tell Milt, then I'm going into town and see the sheriff and Judge Callahan. There must be something they can do. Maybe I'll talk to Doc Doan, too."

"I wish you would," Mary said.

Barney walked on past her, a sickness crawling down into his belly. He had never dreamed he would face a situation like this. He had been aware for several months that Jay had been irrational at times, but it had always been over some trivial thing, or over Rick's behavior, and he hadn't thought much about it. Jay's and Rick's relationship had never been rational anyhow, and as for the trivial things, Barney had laid Jay's performance to his irritation over being crippled up the way he was. Murder was something else.

As he went into the stable, he saw that Curly Klein was the only man there. The others had probably gone into the bunk-house to keep warm. As Barney saddled his bay gelding, Klein walked up to him.

"You ain't going out in this blizzard, are you?" Klein asked.

"I've got to."

Barney glanced at the foreman's face as he tightened the cinch. It was rough-featured and brutal, and reminded Barney that Curly Klein was a dangerous man. He had a good thing with Jay, sucking after him and agreeing with him and doing everything Jay asked him to do. Maybe he knew he would inherit Rainbow if Barney was dead. *If Barney was dead!* A prickle ran down his spine. Klein wouldn't be above killing him if Rainbow was the prize.

"Got to?" Klein shook his head. "Nobody's got to do any such thing. This kind of storm can kill a man."

"Not unless it gets worse," Barney said. "I've got to go see Milt Smith."

Barney mounted and rode out of the stable, Klein closing the door behind him. He rode toward the bridge, the snow pelting his back. Funny thing, Barney told himself. Rick looked at him the same way he looked at Klein. Rick had used almost the same words on him that he had just applied mentally to the foreman: having a good thing, sucking after Jay, agreeing with him, and doing everything he was told.

Now he looked at the situation the same way Rick did. He didn't want Rainbow bad enough to murder Milt Smith for it. He guessed it had taken this kind of a wallop to make him see how it stacked up. He'd go to town first and talk to Doc Doan and Judge Callahan and the sheriff, and see Smith on his way home.

Maybe he'd stop at Mrs. Laird's and visit with Rick for a while. He wanted Rick to know they were on the same side. Maybe something could be done before it was too late if they worked together, something like firing Curly Klein.

The chill that ran down his back as he thought of Klein was not from the cold; it was fear, a kind of gut-level fear he had never known before in his life.

CHAPTER 8

Curly Klein was furious when Monte Bean got back to Rainbow with the news that Rick Proctor was still alive and Scott Shell was probably dead. He threatened to fire Monte on the spot and called him every name he could lay his tongue to.

Klein didn't stop until he ran out of wind. Then he stared at Bean as if he had never seen him before. He said, "I don't know what happened to you, Monte. You used to be the best man I had. You'd do anything I told you, but now you can't do even a simple job."

"I don't know what's the matter with me," Bean said. "We thought Rick was on his way home and we ran out of the stable after him, but that damned Simms must have tipped him off. He was waiting outside for us and got Scott when we were under the lantern. Then Simms cut loose with a scattergun and I took off, thinking Scott was right behind me." He took a long breath, and added, "The next time you get a notion to beef that kid, do it yourself. He's some kind of devil."

"I'll do it before I think of sending you," Klein said in disgust.

"Something else I'd better tell you," Bean said. "Joe Hawks was in the hotel bar last night when Barney came in. Hawks left, but he said something to Barney and went upstairs. Purty soon Barney followed him and they talked in Hawks' room."

"How do you know?"

"I went upstairs after Barney did and listened outside Hawks' door. I couldn't hear all of it, but I heard enough to know that he spilled the whole deal to Barney."

Klein thought about it a moment, then said, "I can handle the old man. I dunno about Barney. If we can't make him see the light, we'll rub him out like we're going to do Rick. We've got too good a deal here to lose it now. Hawks is the one who worries me. He's got to go."

"I'll handle it," Bean said. "I'll take Long John early in the morning and we'll stop the stage after it leaves town."

"And you'd better do something right for a change," Klein said.

Klein was still sleeping when Bean and

Long John Wheeler left near dawn. Now he stood at a small window in the stable watching Barney until he disappeared beyond the curtain of falling snow. He wasn't particularly worried about Barney, although he was curious about why Jay was sending him to see Milt Smith on a day like this. He was worried about Joe Hawks. His testimony could send him and his men to prison for a good part of their lives. If Bean failed again . . .

He didn't. He rode in with Long John a few minutes later. After they'd taken care of their horses and Long John had gone into the bunkhouse, Bean said, "We seen Barney before he seen us and we pulled off the road. Where's he going?"

"Milt Smith's place," Klein said. "Well, are you going to tell me or ain't you?"

"We done the job," Bean said. "We stopped the stage where it started up that sharp pitch on the outer side of Frenchman Creek and took Hawks off. We sent the stage on. We took Hawks down under the bridge and stopped his clock for him. Real comical. He knew what was coming all right. I never seen a man more scared in my life. Maybe we should have taken care of Barney, too. He'll tell Jay. Already told him probably."

"Sure he has, but I can take care of Jay," Klein said. "There'll be time to rub Barney out if we have to."

"I'm gonna go get warm," Bean said. "Coming?"

"Purty soon," Klein said. "I've got some thinking to do. I don't like the way things are stacking up, but I'm glad that damned Rick didn't get together with Hawks. Sooner or later he'll talk to Barney and Barney will tell him, and they'll take a posse to the south range. We're either gonna have to ride off and leave a bonanza or take care of both of 'em. We'll have to find another cattle buyer, too."

"That won't be hard," Bean said.

After Bean left the stable, Klein paced back and forth, his thoughts returning to Barney and why Jay had sent him to see Milt Smith. Jay had been talking for a long time about killing Milt if he didn't sell, and he was just crazy enough to do it. That would blow the lid off. If Jay was sending Barney to warn Milt, somehow he had to stop the old man.

Klein was never one to stand uncertainties. He left the stable and, crossing the yard to the house, knocked on the front door.

Jay yelled, "Come in."

Klein opened the door, slid in, and shut

it. "This is a blow, boss. Worst I've seen for a long time."

"It's a bad one," Jay agreed, motioning to a chair beside him. "Sit down. I wanted to talk to you. I'm glad you came in."

Klein was thoughtful as he wiped his boots on a rug Mary had placed near the door, slapped his hat against his knee, and took off his sheepskin. He hung it on a peg near the door, placed his hat on the peg, and took the chair Jay had indicated.

"I came in to ask about Barney," Klein said. "The storm's getting worse and I figured he ought to be back by now."

"He went to see Milt Smith," Jay said.

"What'd you send him to Smith's for on a day like this?"

If the question had come from anyone but Curly Klein, Jay would have flared back and said it was none of his business, but he never talked that way to Klein. He said, "I'm done waiting on Milt. Barney's gonna tell him he's got twenty-four hours to sell out to me."

"If he don't?"

"Milt knows me, so he knows what'll happen," Jay said as if Klein should know, too. "We'll go down there and burn his place to the ground. We'll shoot him like a dog. He's had his chance."

Klein rolled a cigarette, his eyes on the tobacco and paper. He had burned ranches and shot the owners down like dogs, but somehow this sounded different, coming from Jay Proctor, a respected cowman, a pillar of society, a law-abiding citizen. Klein dismissed it as crazy talk, but something else bothered him.

"I'm wondering why you said 'we.' " Klein reached into a vest pocket for a match. "You expect us to load you into a buckboard and haul you down there so you can run the fireworks?"

"I do if that's what it takes," Jay said harshly. "I shouldn't have to be there. If I give an order, I expect it to be carried out."

"Yeah, sure." Curly scratched his match to life and fired his cigarette. "Just one thing, Jay. It'll be me and Monte and Barney and the rest of us who'll be asking for a rope on our necks. I'll do anything that's reasonable to protect you and Rainbow. I aim to look out for your interest, but Smith ain't giving you no real trouble. What you're fixing to ask us ain't one damn bit reasonable."

Jay stared at him, his face filled with rage. "Well now, by God, I didn't expect that kind of talk from you, Curly. Of course I'll be asking for a rope same as you, except for one fact. I put Harry Osmand into the sheriff's office and he'll do anything I tell him to."

"On most things you'd be dead right," Klein agreed, "but even your own man couldn't stand still for murder. No, you've got to figure out something better, something that will give you what looks like an excuse. We might find some of our calves with the Rafter S brand on 'em in one of Smith's pastures. That's all you'd need."

"I don't need that and I don't need any excuse," Jay said hoarsely. "Looks like I made one hell of a mistake with you. I changed my will a few days ago and fixed it so you were next in line to inherit Rainbow if Barney wasn't alive, but if you're gonna start arguing with everything I say, I'll change it back like it was."

Klein didn't say anything for a full minute. What Jay had just said surprised and shocked him. He knew Jay thought highly of him, but to cut out his younger son Rick in favor of a man who was no blood relation was unbelievable.

"I didn't know that," Klein said in a low tone. "I sure didn't."

"Now maybe you'll start thinking about what you just said," Jay bellowed. "You gonna do what I want or not?"

"I'll do it," Klein said quickly. "You bet I'll do it. I just wanted you to think twice about what you're figuring on doing."

"I've thought more'n twice about it," Jay said bitterly. "I've thought about nothing else for months. He's the only man on the Big Sandy who ain't been reasonable. His outfit is sitting there in the middle of my range. An island! That's what it is, an island, and I ain't putting up with it no longer."

"I savvy that," Klein said. "No, you can't put up with that."

"Now there is one thing," Jay said, "and I want to thresh it out with you right now. I heard this morning that you and some of the crew that you hired have been stealing me blind."

"What? Where'd you pick up a lie like that?"

"Barney told me," Jay said. "He says Joe Hawks told him. Joe claimed he thought you had authority to sell Rainbow stock, so he bought three small herds from you. Now I want to know about it."

"I don't know what to say," Klein said finally, "except that what you heard was a lie, but I don't know why Joe Hawks would tell Barney that. Maybe Barney made up the yarn to get at me. He don't like me. Jealous, I guess."

"I figured it was a lie," Jay said with satisfaction. "I'll get the truth out of Barney when he comes home. Maybe I'll change my will again and make it an even split between you and Barney. Or I might leave it all to you. I don't like being lied to."

"Of course not." Klein rose and, going to the door, put on his coat and hat. "I don't hold this against Barney. Maybe Joe had his reasons for telling a yarn like that. Anyhow, I'm a little fretful about Barney. He should have been back before now."

"Yeah, he should have," Jay agreed, "but you don't need to worry. He's been out in worse storms than this."

"I know he has," Klein agreed, "but he's never shoved Smith around before. Smith ain't gonna like it one bit, Jay. I wouldn't be surprised if he lost his temper and shot Barney. I don't figure that Barney, as easygoing as he is, would expect that."

Jay shook his head. "Milt wouldn't do that. He knows what would happen to him if he did."

"He knows what's going to happen to him anyway," Klein said. "Anyhow, I'll ride over there after dinner just to be sure he's all right."

Jay nodded and said, "You don't need to, but if it'll make your mind easy, go ahead."

Klein opened the door and stepped out into the storm. It was raging as hard as ever, and he didn't relish staying out in it for maybe an hour or more. It could be longer than that. Barney might not be back from Smith's place till late afternoon.

Klein told himself grimly he had no choice. This was a made-to-order situation, and he couldn't afford to miss it.

CHAPTER 9

Barney put his horse in a stable when he reached Proctor City and crossed Main Street to Doc Doan's house. A bell sounded when he opened the front door and stepped into the room that served as the office. The doctor appeared a moment later. He said, "Glad to see you, Barney. Take off your hat and coat and hang 'em up. You look like a snowman."

"I feel like one," Barney said.

Doan stood watching him, his pale blue eyes half closed. After a moment of silence, he said, "A hell of a storm. Funny coming this late in the year. You figure you'll lose any stock?"

Barney nodded. "Probably."

"Well, what can I do for you?" Doan asked. "You look like a healthy specimen."

"I am," Barney said. "I didn't come for no doctoring. I came for advice."

Doan laughed. "Well, I don't charge for

that. As a matter of fact, I could use some myself."

"I've come to a jumping-off place," Barney said, his gaze on the worn carpet. "I'm easygoing, Doc. Went out of my way to get along with that son-of-a-bitch I have for a father. Always done what I was told. Never argued. The obedient son. Well, I can't go on playing that part."

Doan nodded. "I figured you'd come to that conclusion sooner or later. I don't suppose your situation at home is getting any better."

"It's getting worse." Barney swallowed, and then blurted, "Doc, how do you tell if a man's crazy or not?"

"Oooo, that's a tough one," Doan said softly. "I guess there's just no rule of thumb you can go by. In some cases it's easy. Like if a man claims he's Napoleon and goes around with his hand in the front of his shirt. Or if a man sticks a knife into somebody and claims God told him to do it. On the other hand, there's borderline cases where it's hard to know."

"Suppose the man I'm thinking about orders another man to do the knife sticking," Barney said. "Does that mean he's crazy?"

"No, it sure don't," Doan said. "Maybe

he's just mean and smart enough to talk somebody else into doing his dirty work." He jerked a cigar out of his coat pocket and began chewing on it. "I'd say there were cases where a person is crazy who don't stick a knife into somebody else. Take your mother. She's been living in hell for years. Nobody would convict her of murder if she stuck a knife into Jay."

Barney sat down and wiped a hand across his face. "I reckon you knew all the time I was talking about pa. Ma and Rick have been saying he's crazy, but I didn't think so because he's been pretty good to me. Now he's gonna order me or maybe the whole crew to ride to the Rafter S and murder Milt Smith. Today he sent me out in this storm to tell Milt he's got twenty-four hours to sell out to pa. If he don't, we'll kill him. I ain't gonna have nothing to do with his scheming, but when I tell pa, he'll be done with me just like he is with Rick."

"I'm not surprised," Doan said. "Your ma wrote to me, you know. She saw this coming. I had a talk at school with Rick, who said I ought to go see the sheriff. But you know Harry Osmand. I didn't get anywhere. Barney, I don't know what to do. I feel like a man standing under an avalanche and knowing it's coming, but I can't move."

"Pa wasn't like this when I was a boy," Barney said. "What's made him like this?"

"If I knew, I could make medical history," Doan said. "I have a hunch it might be something physical. We've got glands in our body we don't understand. Maybe one of 'em got out of kilter. Or again, maybe it's some kind of emotional pressure."

Doan rose and started pacing around the room. "You're right about him not being this way all his life. Something happened to Jay when he started buying up the other ranches on Big Sandy. The more he got, the more he wanted. He never hated Milt until he tried to buy the Rafter S. The more he wanted it and the harder he tried to buy it, the more stubborn Milt got, and of course each time Jay made an offer and Milt turned it down, the more Jay hated him."

"He's all right about most things," Barney said, "but he goes plumb loco when he starts talking about Milt Smith. I'm supposed to inherit Rainbow. He's cut Rick and ma out of his will. The minute I jump the track, he'll cut me out too."

"Then who gets Rainbow?"

"Curly Klein."

"Oh, he's not that crazy," Doan said as if he couldn't believe it. "I mean, I didn't think he was that far gone."

"To make it worse, Curly's stealing our cattle," Barney said. "This morning I told pa. Right then he believed me, but by the time I get back, he will have talked to Curly and Curly will have pa believing him and thinking I'm the liar."

"He's crazy as a bedbug, all right." Doan threw his partly chewed cigar into a spittoon. "He was crazy when he cussed me the last time I was out to Rainbow. I'm the only doctor in the county, and he'll be in a hell of a fix the next time he needs a doctor. I'll never go out there again."

Doan stopped and jabbed a forefinger at Barney. "You know, there's a lot of human behavior that's crazy, but we're so used to it that we accept it and don't call it crazy. The people who act that way go right on hurting other folks and never get put away where they belong."

"I might as well go home and have it out with pa," Barney said, "then I'll pack up my gear and vamoose. I've got to the end of the line, but leaving won't settle nothing."

"That's right," Doan agreed.

"Chances are he'll get somebody else, Curly probably, to shoot Milt," Barney went on. "I'm going to warn him, but he won't sell to pa and he won't just walk off and leave his spread."

"I dunno," Doan said. "I sure don't. All I know is that you'll never make it stick in court if you try to get Jay declared incompetent. A lot of people like him are shrewd enough to make people think they're rational when they're not."

Barney rose. "I'm going to see Judge Callahan, though I don't figure he'll do anything."

"I'm sorry, Barney," Doan said. "I sure am. I wish your ma would leave Rainbow. Jay might even turn on her."

"I'm afraid he will," Barney said, "but I don't think she'll leave. Rick's tried to talk her into moving to town, but she won't do it."

Barney left the doctor's office, the storm striking him with unabated fury. There was ten inches or more on the ground. It would drift with this wind if it kept up, blocking all the roads around Proctor City.

He climbed the outside stairs to Judge Callahan's office over Houston's hardware store. He had the entire floor, although he didn't need the space. Houston was too tight to put in partitions to make smaller rooms, and Callahan said he wouldn't spend a nickel on another man's property.

Callahan was sitting at his desk at the far end of the room. He had a tremendous fire going in the heater, but the room was cold and the judge was bundled up in a sweater and a robe, with a wool scarf around his neck.

Barney called, "Morning, Judge."

Callahan looked up, saw who it was, and said, "Come on in, Barney, and get warm, if you can get warm in this barn. One of these days, I'm going to speak to Houston about putting up more heat. If he won't, I'll get my own office."

He laughed. It was an idle threat, and both knew it. Barney kept his coat on and spread his hands over the heater.

Callahan was the first to bring up the subject of Jay Proctor. "Well," he said, "I rode out to Rainbow last night like I was ordered. Don't tell me that Jay wants me to go again today?"

"No," Barney said. "Pa told me about the will this morning."

"Good, good," Callahan said. "I told him he ought to tell you."

"I'm leaving home," Barney said. "It'll take more'n his stinking will to make me stay."

"You can't just walk off and leave Rainbow," Callahan said. "It's crazy for you to talk like that."

"That will puts me down as a prime target

for one of Klein's slugs," Barney said. "And now pa sent me to warn Milt Smith that he's got twenty-four hours to sell. I have no choice but to leave."

Callahan shook his head and clucked sympathetically. "No warning was that urgent. But about this slug business. You're saying that Curly would murder you to get Rainbow?"

"Sure he would," Barney said hotly. "It's not me who's crazy. It's pa for not including Rick and ma in the will, and for giving Klein anything. I say pa's the crazy one. Is there any legal way to get him declared incompetent?"

Callahan froze. For a moment he looked as if Barney had said something sacrilegious, then his face turned red. He said thickly, "No way. You're just like that goddam Rick. You go ahead and leave the country. It's the best thing you can do. You don't deserve Rainbow."

Barney had known that Callahan was Jay's man, but he thought Callahan might have some understanding of the problem, or at least have sense enough to see where Jay was heading. He wheeled and stomped out of Callahan's office, knowing that nothing would be gained by arguing with the man.

Barney had intended to see Sheriff Osmand before noon, but now he hesitated, thinking that the sheriff might react exactly the way Callahan had. Then he heard the big clock over the courthouse strike twelve. He knew that he didn't have time to see the sheriff if he wanted to catch Rick at noon.

He turned the corner and strode rapidly through the snow to Mrs. Laird's house.

CHAPTER 10

Rick Proctor was the first out of the high school building. He welcomed the feel of the cold wind on his face, the sting of the snow. He had slept very little the night before, and the morning in school had been hell.

Twice in English class he had dropped off to sleep only to hear his name called. He knew he had been asked a question, but he had no idea what it was. To make it worse, he'd received a zero in geometry because he had failed to do his homework.

Now, striding through the snow to Mrs. Laird's house, he wasn't sure he could stay in school these last weeks and graduate in June with his class. He should be staying with Milt and Ruth Smith. He'd go home this afternoon as soon as school was out, but he wouldn't stay.

He stepped up on Mrs. Laird's porch and kicked the snow off his feet; he opened the door and went into the house, closing the door quickly. Then he stopped, flat-footed, staring at his brother, who stood with his hands extended over the heating stove.

"Barney! What are you doing here?" Rick asked.

Barney hesitated, apparently reluctant to answer the question. He had a strange expression on his face, one that Rick had never seen before. Rick couldn't explain it, but he sensed that Barney had changed. Maybe he was scared; maybe he was just plain mad. Rick wasn't sure, but there was a kind of grimness about Barney, or maybe it was determination, that made him look different.

"I hate to tell you," Barney said finally, "but you've got to know. It's plain goddamn mean trouble. Pa is giving Milt Smith twenty-four hours to sell to him."

Rick nodded, making no effort to appear surprised. He asked, "And then?"

"If Milt won't sell," Barney answered, "pa says we kill him."

"What about Ruth?"

"Pa never said anything about her. Chances are he don't even know she's staying home. Anyway, I'm supposed to warn Milt. I haven't been there yet, but I'll stop by on my way home. I've talked to Doc

Doan and Judge Callahan this morning, and I'll see the sheriff before I leave town. So far I haven't gotten anywhere."

"What are you going to do?"

"I'll go home and tell pa I delivered his message," Barney said glumly, "and then I'll pack my gear and ride out."

"Dinner's on the table, boys," Mrs. Laird called from the kitchen.

Barney took a chair across from Rick, Mrs. Laird sitting at the head of the table. They ate in silence because no one felt like talking.

Finally Rick said, "You might as well tell me what happened. This isn't like you and I don't savvy it, but I'm guessing hell rose up and fell on top of you or you wouldn't be talking like this."

"That's about the size of it," Barney said.

He told Rick about it, including his talks with Doc Doan and Judge Callahan. Finally, he said, "Some things have come clear to me that I just didn't savvy before."

"Like what?"

"First, pa's just as crazy as you'n ma have been telling me. Second, I've been blind and stupid like you've said more'n once. Third, pa don't know what he done because he trusts Klein, but he set me up to be murdered."

"You're dead right on that," Rick agreed sourly. "I'd bet on Klein dry gulching you just as sure as I'd bet on the sun coming up in the morning. But what about ma?"

"Tell her to come and stay with me," Mrs. Laird said. "I've got plenty of room and I'm starved for woman talk. I'd like to have her."

"I don't think she'll do it," Barney said.

"I don't see any way out of this," Rick said, "with Callahan saying we can't get pa declared incompetent."

"Neither do I," Barney said. "Part of the trouble is pa thinks he's God. Sooner or later that's gonna get him. I told him the sheriff wouldn't stand still for murder, but he says the law is Proctor law and Osmand won't touch him."

"Barney, I still ain't real sure why you've jumped the traces the way you have. You had everything lined out the way you wanted it. I don't think pa's gonna live very long. When you get Rainbow, you can fire Klein."

"Damn it, I'm the one that ain't gonna live long," Barney snapped angrily.

So it was fear, Rick thought. He couldn't blame Barney. He'd be afraid, too. But the difference was he'd go ahead and jump Klein, and Barney would be inclined to wait it out, hoping the situation would change or just give up and ride away.

Barney wiped a hand across his face. "I'm sorry, Rick, I didn't aim to say it like that. Sure, I've taken a lot off pa. Klein, too, just so I wouldn't have no trouble. But even a man like me gets shoved to the edge and he's got nowhere to go, so he jumps over. I guess that first it was murdering Milt Smith. I didn't think he'd go that far, but he didn't leave any doubt this morning. The other thing was fixing his will the way he's done. That's crazy even if nothing else was."

Rick finished eating and shoved his plate back. An idea had been shaping up in his mind, but he wasn't sure how far Barney would go to back him up. Barney was upset right now and too mad to know how he really felt. Rick just wasn't sure when the last blue chip was down whether Barney could be as tough as he was talking or not.

"There may be a way to do this," Rick said, "if you're willing to take a chance on getting killed."

"Sure I'll take a chance," Barney said. "I don't want to ride off and leave Rainbow if I can help it. I don't have much money and right now I don't know where I could get a job this time of year."

"The point we've got to work on is that pa's helpless himself," Rick said. "The crew have no loyalty to him. Klein's the one we've got to get. When we do, we pull pa's claws right out by the roots. All he can do is to snort around like a mad bull. If ma won't leave by herself, I guess we'll just have to pick her up and carry her out. Leave pa alone in that house for a few hours and he might not be so crazy. He might even be grateful for what's been done for him."

"Gratitude is something pa ain't got much of," Barney said.

"How many of the crew will stick with Klein in a showdown?" Rick asked.

"He hired six men," Barney said. "I've got a hunch he's known them a long time. Wouldn't surprise me none if they were an outlaw gang that came here to hide out while things cooled off. I figure them six are the ones who stole the cows while Klein gave me and the others something to do on another part of the range."

"If bullets start flying," Rick said, "would all six of them go along with him?"

"I dunno," Barney said. "The only one I'd be sure about is Monte Bean. I think the others would back him, but you can't tell until the ball opens."

"How about the other four that have been with the outfit for years?"

"They'll stay out of it," Barney said.

"I don't suppose they'd back us, either."

"I don't know what the hell you're getting at," Barney said.

"Suppose you ride back here after you see Milt," Rick said. "As soon as I get out of school, I'll come here too. We'll ride out to Rainbow and brace Klein in the bunkhouse. I'm faster than you with a gun. I think I can take Klein. You take Monte Bean. We'll gamble on the others."

"So that's it," Barney said thoughtfully. "All right, we'll tell Klein we're taking the outfit over and he's fired. If he wants to make a fight out of it, he can." Barney rose, shaking his head. "I don't think it'll work, Rick. It'll be us two against seven. That makes purty long odds."

"I don't want to cash in my chips," Rick said, "but I don't want to live like this, either."

"Neither do I," Barney said. "We'll give it a whirl. Thanks for the meal, Mrs. Laird."

"Glad to have you, Barney," she said.

Barney picked up his hat and coat and put them on, then went out into the storm. Rick walked to a window in the front room, watched Barney until he disappeared in the driving snow. Mrs. Laird had followed to stand beside him.

"I'd better get on back to school." Rick turned to get his coat, then swung back.

"Mrs. Laird, you know both of us about as well as anybody except ma. Did you ever think you'd hear Barney talk that way?"

"I never did," she said. "I'm glad I did hear him, though. Some boys are slower to grow up than others. It took Barney a long time."

Rick realized, too late, that he hadn't told Barney about his fight with Monte Bean and shooting Scott Shell, but maybe it was just as well. Barney had enough worries. He put on his coat slowly, a haunting feeling growing in him that he would never see Barney alive again.

CHAPTER 11

Barney found Sheriff Harry Osmand in his office, huddled over a red-hot heating stove. Osmand was a big man, old now and running to fat, but in his day he had been a good lawman. He, like Doc Doan and Judge Callahan, had seen Proctor City change from a post office and store to the town it was now. And, like Callahan, he owed whatever wealth and prestige he had in the community to Jay Proctor.

He glanced up when Barney came in. He grumbled, "You picked a fine day to come to town in."

"I wanted to see you," Barney said. "The weather wasn't my idea."

"I dunno what you wanted to see me about," Osmand said in the same grumbling tone, "but I'll tell you one thing. You ain't getting me out in this storm."

Osmand was cold and grumpy and plainly in no mood to talk, but Barney had no choice. He asked, "Why don't you go home? You can't keep this barn of an office warm."

"You're right about that," the sheriff muttered. "But if you had married my wife, you wouldn't go home either till you had to."

Everybody in the county knew Mrs. Osmand's reputation, and the sheriff never tried to hide the fact that he was a very henpecked man. Barney, knowing this, wished he hadn't asked the question. He walked to the heater and stood with his back to it.

"Sheriff, I'd like to look through your reward dodgers," Barney said.

"Bottom right-hand drawer," Osmand said. "Help yourself." A moment after Barney had lifted the pile of papers to the top of the desk, the sheriff asked, "You got an outlaw treed out there on Rainbow?"

"I'm guessing I have," Barney said as he sat down at the desk and began thumbing through the stack of reward dodgers. "I'm just playing a long hunch, sheriff. I think Curly Klein is a wanted man."

"What?" Osmand whirled around in his swivel chair. "They say in the summertime that it's the heat that gets you, but by hokey, I'd say it's the cold that makes you talk that way."

"I'm not crazy," Barney said, "but pa is or he'd never have hired Klein."

Osmand got up and walked to the desk. "You'd best tell me about it, boy. This kind of talk can get you into a whole passel of trouble."

"I can't be any worse off," Barney said. "I'm in a passel of trouble right now."

He leaned back in his chair and told Osmand what Joe Hawks had said, and then about the will. "If pa wasn't crazy, would he have hired Klein, not knowing anything about him? If he wasn't crazy, would he cut Rick and ma out of the will and name Klein as the next heir? If he wasn't crazy, would he fix it so I'm the only one who stands between Klein and Rainbow?"

"Well, by God," Osmand said, "I knew he was getting mighty boogery about some things, but I didn't know all this."

"You didn't know that he's sending me to warn Milt Smith that he's got twenty-four hours to sell out to him or we're going down there and kill him?"

"No, I didn't," Osmand said, "but I guess I ain't surprised, after hearing him talk the way he has for several months."

"And you hadn't heard that pa says the law in this county is Proctor law and you wouldn't touch us if we shoot Milt?"

Osmand sat down hard and rubbed the top of his bald head. "Well, he is crazy. I owe him a lot, and I'd do a lot to please him, but I couldn't overlook murder." Then he shrugged. "Maybe it's just talk. You wouldn't follow up any orders like that, would you?"

"No."

"He sure can't do nothing in that wheelchair of his," Osmand said. "I guess it's nothing to get hot about."

"You'd better get hot about it," Barney said. "You think Klein wouldn't do it, knowing what the will says?"

Osmand got up and began to pace back and forth across his office. He wheeled to face Barney. "When did Klein ride in here?"

"Three years ago this spring," Barney said. "Pa was short of help right then and he was impressed with Klein's toughness. That fall our old foreman, Jiggs Magoo, got stomped on by his horse and couldn't ride no more, so pa hired Klein to rod the outfit. After that, six men rode in looking for work. Klein hired every one of 'em."

"And fired six of the old hands," Osmand said. "It wasn't all in a bunch, I recollect. They came stringing in one at a time. Must have been over a year. I remember how the old hands kicked up some dust when they got fired. They were all purty sore about it."

"They had a right to be," Barney said. "I

never got the straight of it, but I always figured Klein lied about 'em to pa, and pa took Klein's word. Anyhow, six of his men are in the Rainbow crew."

"I remember something," Osmand said thoughtfully, "now that you've brought all of this up. There was a big bank robbery in New Mexico just before Klein showed up here. A mine payroll, I think it was mostly."

"How many men did it?"

"Eight, but one got killed and a couple more were wounded," Osmand answered. "It don't prove nothing, though. The men wore masks and we don't even have a description of 'em. I mean, of their size or what their horses looked like or anything. Two bank tellers were killed, and folks got too excited and scared to remember much of what the robbers looked like."

Barney finished going through the reward dodgers and put them back into the desk drawer. "Nothing there," he said.

Osmand changed the subject. "I don't know about declaring a man crazy. You'll have to see Judge Callahan —"

"I have and he says no," Barney interrupted.

"I ain't surprised," Osmand said grimly. "The judge has got a good thing going with your pa, the will changing and deeds for new property and lawsuits of one kind or another." He shook his head. "Jay's been doing some crazy things, but murdering Milt Smith, why, even the judge couldn't stomach that."

"Suppose you came out to Rainbow," Barney said, "and told pa you draw the line at murder. Maybe he'd back off if you told him you'd be out here the minute you heard Milt had been killed and pa would be the first man you'd arrest?"

"I'll try in the morning," Osmand said. "But do you think Jay would listen to me?"

"No, I don't," Barney admitted. "I think he's stopped listening."

"That's the way I figger it," Osmand said uneasily, "but I'll try. Anyhow, this is my last term."

Barney rose. "I'll get along and see Milt."

"I'll be out to Rainbow in the morning," Osmand said, his mouth puckered as if he had just eaten something that had a bad taste.

"Good," Barney said.

He left the sheriff's office, thinking there was no use to tell Osmand that he wouldn't be there, or that he and Rick were going after Klein this afternoon. At least he'd started Osmand thinking.

He got his horse from the livery stable and

turned toward the Rafter S. The storm had abated now. Snow was still in the air, but the flakes were spiraling down instead of being driven by the wind. The temperature was about the same, Barney thought, but it seemed much warmer because the wind had slacked off.

He dismounted in front of the Smith house and tied his horse. Then for a moment he simply stood there. He would rather have taken a whipping, he told himself, than to go through with this; but Milt had to be warned. After that it would be up to him.

Barney walked up the path to the porch, kicked the snow from his boots, and knocked.

Ruth opened the door at once, saying, "Come in, Barney." As soon as he was inside, she said, "I saw you standing out there beside your horse like you were scared to come in."

"I was," he said.

She laughed softly as if the idea was ridiculous. She said, "I'm almost your sister or will be as soon as school's out unless Rick changes his mind, so you shouldn't —"

"He won't change his mind," Barney said. "Where's Milt?"

"He's out back," she said. "I was hoping you came to see me."

"When I call on a girl, it'll be one who's not taken," Barney said. "Go get your pa, will you?"

He knew he was being curt, but he was in no mood to banter. She stared at him a moment, the smile leaving her lips, then she nodded and disappeared into the kitchen. He heard the back door open, heard her call her father, then she returned to the kitchen and shut the door. But she did not rejoin Barney in the front room.

Milt came in a moment later. He was rubbing his red cheeks and shaking his head. He said, "Howdy, Barney. By grab, it feels warmer, but the thermometer says it's hanging right there at ten." He motioned toward the kitchen. "Come on back. We didn't build a fire out here today, but the kitchen's warm."

"No, I can tell you mighty quick what I came for," Barney said, "but I wish to hell I didn't have to say it. Pa sent me to tell you that you had twenty-four hours to sell to him or he'll send his men to kill you."

Milt's face turned gray. "You gonna be riding with those men?" he asked.

"You know I won't. I've done what pa told me all my life, and I never thought I'd buck him, but by God, this is too much. I'm meeting Rick back in town as soon as he gets out of school, but I don't know whether we can stop pa or not. I figure Curly Klein and his bunch will be here tomorrow."

"We'll be ready for 'em," Milt said. "We've got a purty good fort here. They might burn us out, but I guess they won't do that tomorrow, wet as it is with all this snow."

"Milt, I know you ain't gonna sell," Barney said, "but you ought to move into town for a few days."

"No," Milt shot back. "We'll hang and rattle."

Ruth had come into the room. She asked, "What are you and Rick up to? We don't want either one of you getting killed on our account."

"It won't be on your account," Barney said. "It'll be on our account. Anyhow, you know me. I never take any chances."

"I thought I knew you," she said, "but I guess I don't know the Barney I'm talking to today."

"I've got to get back to town," Barney said. "So long."

"So long," Milt said.

Ruth didn't say anything, but she lifted a hand and waved to him. She was about to cry, he thought, and began to curse his father as he stomped through the snow to his horse. The world was tough even when everything went the way it should. Bad enough that things happened that were beyond a man's control: storms like this one and fires and epidemics and droughts, but for a man like Jay Proctor to raise hell and make people suffer just for a crazy whim was more than any human should or could put up with.

He mounted and rode back the way he had come, the bank of the Big Sandy to his left. He thought about his younger brother and Ruth and how much Jay could do for them and wouldn't. Suddenly, without warning, a powerful blow slammed him in the back.

He heard a shot and then a second one, and felt himself falling and falling. The cold of the snow was all around him; he tried to crawl out of it, but there was no strength in his arms and legs. A moment later his face fell into the snow. Then there was nothing.

CHAPTER 12

Klein left Rainbow as soon as he could saddle up after his talk with Jay. All the way to the bridge he was plagued by a feeling he had been too slow, that Barney would have delivered his warning to Milt Smith before now and would meet him between the house and the river.

He crossed the long bridge over the Big Sandy without seeing anyone and breathed a sigh of relief as he turned south toward Smith's Rafter S. When he could see the house ahead of him through the driving snow, he reined up, wondering if Barney was inside.

Klein turned off the road down the steep bank to the stream bed, forcing his mount through the deep snow where it had drifted against the east bank of the stream. He dismounted, studied the brush above him, and decided it was thick enough to screen him when Barney rode past if he stayed flat.

Sooner or later Barney had to go by.

Klein wasn't satisfied as he tramped back and forth in the snow that covered the sand at the edge of the stream. Barney was not a close friend of Milt Smith's, and the girl belonged to Rick, so what in hell was he taking so long for?

As the minutes piled up into an hour or more, Klein became impatient. He couldn't go in after Barney. All he could do was to wait, and the longer he waited, the worse the nagging fear became that Barney wasn't in the house. But Jay had sent him here. He couldn't be anywhere else.

Then, with the storm dying down, he saw Barney riding toward him from the north. Apparently he had gone to town! Why? Klein had no answer to this. Barney didn't have the gumption to take things into his own hands and see the sheriff. Or Judge Callahan.

Still, the thought bothered Klein. He knew he could handle Callahan. He wasn't so sure of Osmand. Barney must have gone to see one or both of them. He didn't like Rick well enough to spend all this time visiting with him. Besides, Rick would have been in school.

The chance that he had ridden into town for a drink in a storm like this wasn't to be

120

considered. Nobody in his right mind would do that, least of all Barney Proctor. No, he must have gone to see Sheriff Osmand and had dropped the whole business in his lap. Klein wasn't sure what might come of that.

He swore in disgust. He was cold and hungry and he had wasted close to two hours waiting when there had been nothing to wait for. Barney had outsmarted him without even knowing what he'd done.

Klein had to admit that he had underestimated Barney. If he had been to see Osmand, he must have some idea of how to avoid raiding Smith's ranch and killing him, but he probably hadn't had the guts to tell Jay to his face that he wanted no part of this business.

Klein watched him ride by him and go on to the Smith house. He dismounted, tied his horse, and waded through the snow to the front door. At least Klein now knew his man was here. Maybe he wouldn't stay long.

He was relieved a few minutes later to see Barney leave the house. He climbed the bank and lay on his belly in the snow. With the leaves gone from the willows, there wasn't enough of a screen along the bank to hide him. He had no choice but to get down in the snow and stay there motionless.

He checked his gun and waited, breathing

softly. This was an old game to Curly Klein. He had played it often enough, yet it seemed different today. He guessed it was just that more was at stake than when he was killing for someone else at so much a head.

Barney rode by. As soon as he was past, Klein tipped his gun up and fired. The bullet knocked Barney out of his saddle. Klein fired a second time as Barney was falling and knew he missed, but he was sure the first shot had done the trick.

He waited a moment, tempted to take a close look at Barney, but the Smiths likely had heard the shot and would be watching from a window. Not that anybody would believe Milt Smith, but it was just as well not to give Rick or the sheriff or anyone else the slightest bit of evidence against him.

He led his horse downstream until he was sure he was far enough away so neither Milt nor Ruth would see him if he was on his horse. He stepped into the saddle and followed the stream bed for another quarter of a mile, then he found a low place in the bank where the snow was not drifted as high as in most places and spurred his horse up the sharp pitch to the road.

Crossing the bridge, he rode as fast as he could through the deep snow to Rainbow. He reined up in front of the bunkhouse and went in. Most of the men were playing poker. Several, including Monte Bean, were sprawled out on their bunks.

The men glanced at him questioningly as he came in, but he wasted no time. He said, "Monte, you and Long John harness up a team and go fetch Barney's body in. Milt Smith shot him about fifty yards or so on this side of his house. He's in the road."

He wheeled around and walked out quickly, ignoring the questions that were thrown at him. He mounted and rode to the house. He knocked on the front door and went in before Jay could call to him.

"I hate to tell you this, Jay," Klein said, "but you're going to have to know. Milt Smith shot and killed Barney after he left Smith's house. I guess Barney's warning must have made him loco. I'm going into town to notify Osmand. There shouldn't be no trouble convicting Smith. I've sent Monte and Long John after the body."

He heard Mrs. Proctor cry out from the kitchen; he saw Jay's face turn white with shock. Klein wheeled and strode to the front door, not stopping when Jay recovered enough to bellow, "Forget Osmand. Take the boys down there and settle this right now."

Klein left the house, shutting the door

behind him. He mounted his horse and quickly rode to town. His first stop was at the sheriff's office. Without preamble, he said, "Sheriff, Barney Proctor was shot and killed by Milt Smith this afternoon. The body will be at Rainbow if you want to see it, but you'd better go bring Smith in."

Osmand was standing with his back to his heating stove. He blinked and shook his head, then said, "I don't believe it. Barney was in here just a little while ago."

"I don't care if you believe it or not," Klein snapped. "I told you what happened. Now go bring Smith in and lock him up. Jay ain't gonna stand still for Barney getting beefed and you know it."

"Just how do you know Milt shot Barney?" Osmand demanded. "Did you see him do it?"

"No, I didn't see him," Klein answered angrily. "Maybe he told you that Jay sent him to warn Smith to sell within the next twenty-four hours. I found the body in the road about fifty yards north of Smith's house. He had been to see Smith and was coming back when he was murdered. Now who else is there who would shoot Barney under those circumstances but Smith? Barney had no enemies. You know that."

Osmand turned from the heater to face

Klein. He said, "I'll think on it, Curly."

"No, by God," Klein said, exasperated. "You got no need to think on it. Just go out there and arrest Smith. If you don't, Jay will have him lynched."

Klein turned and stomped out of the sheriff's office, as angry as he had ever been in his life. Osmand hadn't exactly defied him, but he hadn't said he'd arrest Smith, either. Klein had a hunch Osmand had no intention of bringing the man in.

He'd done all he could, Klein thought as he headed for Judge Callahan's office. As he climbed the stairs, he told himself that Jay would be giving all kinds of wild orders if the sheriff didn't arrest Smith, and that would put Klein in a tough position. Either he would carry out Jay's orders and get into trouble with the law, or he'd defy Jay and lose the biggest windfall of his life.

He opened the door of Callahan's office and went in quickly.

Callahan glanced up and nodded. "Howdy, Curly," he said. "I guess this is visiting day from Rainbow. Barney was in while ago."

"He won't be in again," Klein said as he crossed the room to the judge's desk. "Milt Smith shot and killed him this afternoon."

"The hell he did," Callahan said, deeply

shocked. "How'd it happen?"

"I wasn't there when he was shot," Klein said, "but Barney warned Smith to leave within the next twenty-four hours. I guess this was Smith's way of telling Jay he wasn't going to sell."

"A highly effective manner of getting his answer across." Callahan leaned back in his chair and chewed on his cigar, a sly grin coming to his thin-lipped mouth. "Well now, Curly, that leaves you the high cock-a roarem, doesn't it? Or has Jay told you about his will."

Klein nodded. "Jay told me this morning. Of course he may change his will again and leave the outfit to Rick or his wife or both."

Callahan shook his head. "He won't do anything of the kind. My advice goes a long way with Jay. I would never advise him to leave anything to Rick after the way the boy has treated him. As far as Mary's concerned, what would she know about running a big outfit like Rainbow? No, I think Jay will leave everything the way it is." He paused, and added, "Providing, of course, he gets the proper cooperation from you."

"He'll get it," Klein said. "And I need to remember that there is always a good chance a man in his physical condition will not live long."

"I was thinking of that," Callahan said blandly. "A son like Rick might murder him sometime, not knowing what the will says."

They laughed, and Klein said, "You son-of-a-bitch."

"I judge you to be the same caliber of a son-of-a-bitch," Callahan said.

"I wouldn't want to be any smaller caliber," Klein said. "If and when I own Rainbow, I'll need a lawyer. One with position in the community, maybe one who has been a judge."

"I'll remember that," Callahan said.

"I'd better be getting back," Klein said. "I told Osmand to bring Smith in, but he didn't act like he was going to. He's got to or I'll be in a hell of a bind."

"I'll drop over and give him a nudge," Callahan said.

Klein left the judge's office, knowing he should notify Rick, but not wanting to. He mounted, deciding to leave a message with Mrs. Laird. Later, as he approached Mrs. Laird's house, he saw Rick turning in at her gate.

"Rick," Klein called and touched up his horse.

Rick turned, recognized Klein, and stopped, making no effort to hide the hostility he felt for the Rainbow foreman. He waited, not saying a word.

When Klein reached him, he reined up and said, "Your brother was shot and killed this afternoon by Milt Smith. You'd better get out to Rainbow."

Klein rode on, not wanting to carry on a conversation with Rick any more than Rick wanted to talk to him. He'd find a way to get the kid out of the way, he thought savagely. Callahan had hinted at a good solution. Kill Jay and frame Rick for it. Right now he didn't have any idea how to go at it, but he'd think of something.

He was still turning it over in his mind when he reached Rainbow. The wagon was drawn up by the barn, and Monte Bean and Long John had just finished unharnessing the horses when Klein led his horse into his stall.

"Jay say anything when you took the body into the house?" Klein asked.

"What body?" Bean said in an irritated tone. "I don't know why you sent us on a wild-goose chase in this weather. There wasn't any body."

Klein froze. It was impossible. He turned to stare at Bean who stood in the runway behind him. "Did his horse come in?"

Bean nodded. "He was here when I got back."

There could be only one answer. Smith must have moved the body — but why? Klein had no answer to that question unless Smith thought having the body in the house would keep Jay and his crew off his back.

There was a slim chance that Barney was still alive, but Klein didn't believe that. Either way, he was going to have to go into Smith's house and fetch Barney to Rainbow. If Barney was alive when they left Smith's place, he wouldn't be when they got home.

CHAPTER 13

Ruth Smith had started to make a cake. Her father had poured a cup of coffee and was standing by the cook stove drinking it when they heard the shots. They straightened, looked at each other, and Milt cried out, "Barney."

He set his coffee cup on the kitchen table and ran to a window in the front room, Ruth a step behind him. Milt couldn't see Barney, but his riderless horse was galloping down the road. He wheeled to face Ruth, who was peering out of another window.

"He must be down in the snow," Milt said. "I'll harness up the team and hook up the wagon. Bring some blankets."

Grabbing his hat and sheepskin off the antler rack near the door, he ran outside, buttoning his coat as he ran. The wind had almost stopped and the snow had diminished to just a few flakes that drifted downward, but the sky still held the cold, gray look of snow. Milt told himself the storm wasn't through.

By the time he had harnessed the horses and hooked them up to the wagon, Ruth had come out of the house with an armload of blankets. She threw them into the wagon bed and climbed onto the seat. Milt was already there. As soon as Ruth was seated, he yelled at the horses and sent them down the road on the run.

They found Barney about seventy-five yards from the house lying on his face at the edge of the road. He wasn't moving. Milt jumped down, noticing that Barney had pulled himself through the snow for several feet, his blood making a red splotch in the white. Milt saw that a bullet had gone into Barney's back between his shoulder blades. He turned Barney over, but Milt couldn't tell if he was alive or not.

"Well?" Ruth asked.

"I don't know." Milt picked up a wrist and felt for the pulse, then shook his head. "He's alive, but that's about all. His pulse is mighty weak."

He lifted Barney and laid him carefully in the wagon bed. Ruth covered him with blankets and knelt beside him so she could hold the blankets in place. Milt stepped onto the seat and turned the wagon back toward the house. This time he drove carefully, afraid that a hard jolt would start the bleeding.

The trip back to the house took only a few minutes, but it seemed an age to Milt. He asked himself who would try to kill Barney, but he couldn't think of anyone who would do it. The whole business seemed crazy. If Jay or any of his crew had come here to kill anybody, they'd try to get him. Barney had only brought the warning that Milt had expected.

He stopped the team close to the front door. Stepping down, he lifted Barney from the wagon and carried him inside, Ruth following with the blankets. As they went through the door, she called, "Put him in my room."

Milt laid him down. He said, "Heat some irons. He's cold enough to be dead."

She ran into the kitchen as Milt pulled off Barney's boots and socks, then gently removed his shirt and pants and covered him with the blankets. The wound was oozing blood, but not as fast as Milt expected. He stepped back and looked at Barney as Ruth came into the room.

"Don't look to me like he has much chance," Milt said. "His face has got a gray look I don't like."

"You've got to go get Doc Doan," Ruth said.

Milt hesitated. "I know I do, and you can do more for him than I can, but I don't like to leave you after what Rick said last night and then what Barney said this afternoon."

"I'll be fine," she said impatiently. "He's got to have the doctor."

"All right," Milt said reluctantly. "You get them irons around him as soon as they're hot. Keep heating some so you can change them. Bar the door as soon as I leave. You'd better have some boiling water on the stove when Doc gets here."

She nodded. "Don't fuss, pa. Now go on."

He turned and walked out of the room, stopping by the door long enough to buckle his gunbelt around him. He drove the team to the barn, unharnessed the horses, and saddled his black gelding, the fastest horse he had. Although with the snow as heavy as it was, he knew he couldn't make very good time.

The snow had not drifted a great deal on the road, so he wasn't held up as much as he had expected. He stopped at Mrs. Laird's to tell Rick, but Rick wasn't there. He told Mrs. Laird what had happened and asked her to tell Rick. He went on to Doc Doan's house and told him about Barney.

"I'll harness my mare right away," Doan said. "Got any idea who did it?"

Milt shook his head.

"I have," Doan said grimly, but he didn't identify his suspect. He put on his coat and hat and grabbed up his black bag. "Ride around to the back, Milt."

A moment later Doan rushed out through the back door and ran to his barn. Milt waited in the alley until Doan backed his mare out of her stall and hooked up to the buggy.

"You go ahead if you can travel faster'n I can," Doan said.

"No, I'll stick with you," Milt said. "I've got a notion that if whoever shot Barney found out he wasn't dead, he'd try again. One way to make sure he dies is to see that you don't get there."

"Nobody would bother me," Doan said, but Milt had a feeling that the old doctor was glad to have him riding beside his buggy.

When they reached the house, Milt said, "Go on in, Doc. I'll take care of your horse."

Doan nodded, picked up his black bag, and ran into the house. Milt drove the buggy to the barn, unharnessed the mare, and led her inside and tied her in a stall. He went back for his horse and put him in the barn, his gaze whipping around the out-buildings and road and the brush along the river before he went into the barn. There was no sign of movement anywhere on the white earth, but that fact brought no comfort to Milt.

It was just so damned easy to bushwhack a man, he thought bitterly. Anybody could have shot Barney in the back. Only a coward would kill a man that way, but the world was full of cowards who hated other people enough to kill them. That was where Milt could not make any sense out of Barney's shooting. The man was not hated by anyone as far as Milt knew.

He went into the house, knocked the snow off his boots, and took off his hat and coat. Ruth was with Doan in her bedroom, working on Barney. No use to bother them, Milt thought, and went on into the kitchen. He dropped his hat and coat over a chair and poured a cup of coffee. He stood by the stove, shivering, not so much from the cold as from a sudden, chilling fear.

Last night he had discounted Rick's warning, and he had thought even less of Barney's this afternoon, putting them down as the raving threats of a madman. But shooting and killing went beyond threats, and now Milt realized that a madman was far more dangerous than a sane one.

Barney's shooting must somehow be related to Jay's goading ambition and threats, but the more Milt thought about it, the less sense it made. Jay would not order the murder of his own son, particularly the one who had been loyal to him. The point was, of course, that if someone was in the country who was capable of killing Barney, he would be equally capable of killing Milt Smith.

For the first time Milt seriously considered selling the Rafter S. Then his natural stubbornness took over. He knew he would die here before he would bow to Jay. Ruth was another matter, and he remembered what Rick had said last night. He'd better send her to town, he decided reluctantly.

Doc Doan and Ruth came into the kitchen, the doctor plainly troubled. He met Milt's gaze and shook his head. "I got the bullet out," he said, "and I don't think he's got any broken bones or damage to his vital organs, but just getting that slug into his body and lying there in the snow was hard on him. He lost some blood, though I don't think it was enough to hurt him."

Ruth poured a cup of coffee for the doctor. He took it and pulled a chair up to the stove and sat down.

"Is he conscious?" Milt asked.

Doan nodded. "Sort of. He groaned and muttered a few words I couldn't make out. I gave him something to make him sleep. Nothing to do except keep him quiet and warm and let his body do the healing while we hope he don't get pneumonia." He stirred his coffee, staring thoughtfully at the black liquid. "There's something else I don't savvy. He's worse off than he ought to be with the kind of a wound he's got. His blood pressure's very low and his pulse is damned feeble. You know, maybe he don't want to get well."

"I wouldn't blame him," Ruth said.

"I've been figuring on it," Milt said, "and I can't think of anyone who would do this."

"I can," Doan said. "I don't have any proof, but I'm sure it was Curly Klein. You don't know about the will?"

Milt shook his head and Doan told him, adding, "I don't know how much of a bad man Klein is, but I've got a hunch he's bad all the way down to his toes. Killing Barney makes him next in line for Rainbow, and then he'll find a way to kill Jay. You'll see."

"Well then," Ruth said, "Barney doesn't have much reason to get well. To work like he had for his dad and then have a will that makes Klein next in line, why, it's the same as murdering Barney himself."

Milt turned to Ruth. "Rick was dead right about you staying here. I hadn't thought it was serious, but you can't get much more serious than trying to kill a man. I want you to go into town and stay with Mrs. Laird."

She shook her head. "I guess I never disobeyed you before in my life, pa, but I am now. I'm staying right here. I have to nurse Barney."

Milt realized this was her way of getting around saying she was going to help take care of him. This was no time to take pride in his stubbornness, Milt told himself, or to quarrel with her. Rick would be along soon. Maybe he could persuade her to leave the Rafter S until the trouble was over, but he didn't really believe it.

"All right," he said.

Ruth glanced at him, surprised that he surrendered so easily and wondering if it was a trick. She shrugged as if deciding not to press it, then asked, "You told Rick about Barney?"

"Rick wasn't there, but I told Mrs. Laird and she promised to tell him."

"Then he'll be here any time," she said. "If he offers to stay this time and help fight, let him. He won't consider Rainbow his outfit now."

"His mother is the only problem," Doan said. "Somehow he's got to get her out of that house." He set his cup on the table. "I'd better get back to town before the storm starts again. Nothing more I can do here. Ruth can keep him warm and quiet and feed him if he's hungry."

"I'll bring your mare and buggy to the front door," Milt said. "You might as well stay by the stove and keep warm as long as you can."

"All right," Doan said. "I'm not looking forward to driving home, and I'm not looking forward to coming back tomorrow, but I will unless the storm gets too bad to travel in or the snow drifts so I can't get here."

Milt put on his hat and picked up his coat. He glanced at Ruth as if thinking of asking her once more to go to town. She could ride with Doan. But she must have sensed what was in his mind because she frowned and shook her head at him.

He slipped into his coat and buttoned it as he crossed the kitchen and front room, then opened the door and stepped outside. He glanced casually at the barn, then at the road to the north. He jumped back inside and slammed the door, his heart pounding.

"Bar the back door, Ruth," he yelled as he

dropped the heavy bar across the front door. "We've got visitors."

CHAPTER 14

Monte Bean and Long John Wheeler had started toward the bunkhouse when Klein called, "Monte, come back here."

Irritated, Bean turned to face Klein, but Long John didn't break his stride. If anything, he moved faster, as if afraid Klein was going to call him back, too.

"Well?" Bean asked.

"Saddle your horse," Klein said. "We're going to call on Smith. He must have moved Barney's body into the house. We've got to find out. Likewise we've got to find out if he's still alive. I don't think he is, but we've got to make sure."

"I ain't doing no such thing," Bean shouted angrily. "By God, I'm froze to death now. If you think I'm gonna . . ."

"I think you are," Klein said grimly. "You're in this as deep as I am, and we'll either swing together or ride out of here a couple of rich men. Only you won't live long enough to be a rich man if you don't do what I tell you. Now, saddle up!"

For a moment Bean didn't move. He met Klein's stare, rebellion boiling up in him. He said sullenly, "You don't need me to call on Milt Smith."

"I need you, all right," Klein said. "I don't think he's got the guts to pull a trigger on me, but I know he won't do it if there's two of us."

Bean continued to meet Klein's gaze, his anger smoldering instead of flaming high as it had for a moment. He had never been able to stand against Klein, and he couldn't now. Shrugging, he strode toward the barn. He was a weak one, Klein told himself sourly and wondered why he'd put up with the man as long as he had. Well, it wouldn't be much longer. They'd milk this situation dry and be on their way. He'd find a way to get rid of Bean when the time came.

He waited until Bean led his horse out of the stable, then he mounted and jerked his head for the other man to follow.

Bean pulled in beside him, asking, "Just how do you expect to get into Smith's house to talk to him? He knows by now what old Jay's up to. It don't make no difference whether there's one or two of us. He'll shoot our tails off before he lets us in."

"Maybe not," Klein said. "He knows that when we come to finish him, we'll bring the whole crew. I figure he'll talk, just on the off chance he can put off a showdown."

"I hope so," Bean said sourly. "A showdown might finish us around here, even if Jay orders it." He paused, then added bitterly, "You sure pick the damnedest weather to send me gallivanting all over the country. Right now nothing seems important except to get warm."

"You'll get plenty warm in hell if we don't handle this thing right," Klein snapped. "If we wasn't playing for big stakes, I'd say to hell with the whole business, but we've got a ripe peach ready to pick off the tree and we're gonna pick it."

After that they rode in silence. The sky was clearing and the wind had died down, but the temperature was dropping steadily. They'd lost some stock, all right, Klein told himself bitterly, and now for the first time he thought of the cattle as his, not Jay Proctor's. For just a moment he saw himself as a respectable rancher owning Rainbow and filling Jay's big boots.

His dream vanished as quickly as it had come. He had been here too long now. If he stayed much longer, his past was bound to catch up with him. He'd hang on just long enough to clean the range of Rainbow cattle. If he owned the outfit, no one would question what he did. The only problem was time. Three years was too long for a wanted man to stay put.

So far he had not attracted any particular attention, but once Jay Proctor was killed and he inherited Rainbow, that would change. Well, there was only so much he could do to hurry things along. He still hadn't figured out how to frame Rick for his father's murder, but there had to be a way. He'd think of it.

They reached the Smith house, reined up, and dismounted. Klein gazed at the house for a moment, then waded through the snow to the front door, Bean following. Klein knocked. There was no answer. He knocked again, drumming his knuckles hard against the door. Still no answer.

"Maybe they went to town," Bean said, "where it's warm and safe."

Klein shook his head. "Not a stubborn old goat like Milt Smith. He'll never give up till he's dead." He chewed on his lower lip a moment, then shouted, "I want to talk to you, Smith. Let us in."

"I've got no need to talk to you," Smith yelled. "Get on your horses and slope out of here."

"Look," Klein said impatiently. "If we aimed to make trouble, we'd have brought the whole crew along and we'd do our talking with guns, but I don't want trouble no more'n you do. That's why me'n Monte are here."

"Talk away," Smith said.

"I ain't talking to no man through a closed door," Klein said. "Not on a day as cold as this one. Now let us in, damn it."

For a time Smith was silent, then Klein heard a woman say, "Don't do it, pa."

That would be the girl, Ruth. Klein thought she was spunky, and smarter than her old man. One thing about Rick Proctor. He had good taste in a woman. Klein had made a few advances in her direction, but she had wanted no part of him. Well, she deserved anything she got. If she'd treated him differently, he'd have seen to it that Milt wasn't under the gun the way he was now.

The door opened, and Smith stepped back, a shotgun covering Klein. He said, "Come in and shut the door. I wouldn't leave a dog outside in this kind of weather."

Klein stepped into the house, Bean following. He glanced around the living room as Bean shut the door. Ruth was not in sight. A door on the far side of the room was open. Klein guessed that it led into the kitchen. He moved toward it, stopping only when Smith motioned with the barrel of the shotgun.

"That's far enough," Smith said. "Say what you've got to say and git. If you're singing the same song about me selling out or getting burned out or killed, I say to hell with you."

Klein stopped. He was close enough to the door to see that it did indeed open into the kitchen. The only person in the room was Doc Doan, who was sitting in a rocking chair in front of the big range. Ruth was nowhere in sight.

There were doors on both ends of the living room that likely led into bedrooms. Ruth was probably in one, and Barney's body would be in the other one. But right now the question that hit Klein was why Doc Doan was here.

The possibility that Barney was still alive and Smith had gone after Doan to tend the wounded man jarred Klein. He should have made sure Barney was dead before he left him, but that was useless thinking. The chance was gone.

Klein jammed his hands into his pockets to show Smith he had no intention of drawing his gun. He asked, "What's Doc Doan doing out here in weather like this?"

"Ruth went after him for me," Smith said. "My heart's been kicking up and she got worried. If Jay keeps pushing me, I may save him the trouble of shooting me, but I figure Ruth will hang as tight as I have."

"Then we wouldn't be no better off, would we?" Klein scratched his chin, thinking that this explanation was logical. Milt Smith had had enough pressure on him to bring a heart attack on any man. "I'm not singing that old song, Smith. I don't like the way things are stacking up no more than you do. Jay's as loco as they come. Doc can bear that out. Anyhow, Jay means what he says. You've made it worse by beefing Barney."

He spoke loud enough for Doan to hear. It was a good thing for the medico to hear it. He had no way of knowing how his words hit the doctor, but he saw that they staggered Milt Smith.

The rancher stared blankly at him, his eyes wide, his mouth springing open. Then he took a long breath and said softly, "You son-of-a-bitch! So you told Jay I'd shot his boy. Is that it?"

"That's it," Klein said.

"All right," Smith flung at him, "you go ahead and tell the sheriff and see if he thinks

I done it."

"I already told him," Klein said. "He'll be along to jail you. I figured he'd be here before now."

"What makes you think I shot Barney?" Smith asked.

"Jay sent him to warn you to sell or take the consequences," Klein said. "It's purty plain to me you let him come in and talk, then you took after him and shot him just to show Jay you were going to hang tough. I heard the shot and rode this way far enough to see the body, then I lit a shuck for Rainbow, told Jay, and sent Monte and Long John to fetch Barney. When they got here, the body was gone. You're the only one who could have got it. I guess you figgered to get rid of it later so the sheriff wouldn't have any evidence."

"You're dead wrong," Smith said. "It's my guess you're the one who shot Barney."

"I ain't the one who's in a squeeze from old Jay," Klein said. "You are."

He had been edging toward the door on the south wall, driven by the possibility that Barney was still alive in one of the bedrooms. He had to be sure. He didn't think Smith would use his shotgun unless he was backed into a corner, and Klein had no intention of doing that. Still, he had to be careful. He had learned long ago that it was foolish to judge a man until he had been tested.

He was within five feet of the door before Smith said, "Damn it, Klein, stand still. I don't want to give you a load of buckshot, but I will if you make me."

"I ain't making you," Klein said, "and you won't pull the trigger if you want to stay alive. Monte would smoke you down before you could take another breath. I told you I didn't want no trouble. I just aim to see for myself whether Barney's body is here."

He lunged toward the door and turned the knob, counting on his sudden move and the threat of Monte Bean's gun to keep Smith quiet. One or the other or both worked because Smith yelled at him and that was all he did.

Klein yanked the door open, then stood motionless, his breath going out of him. Ruth, standing beside a bed that was piled high with clothes, had her back to him. She was completely naked. Klein had not been sure what he'd see, but it certainly wasn't this.

Ruth whirled to face him when she heard the door. Her face was bright red, and for a moment she was too furious and embarrassed to say anything. Then she found her voice.

"You bastard," she screamed. "Get out and shut the door, damn it."

She grabbed a boot off the bed and threw it at him. If he hadn't ducked, he'd have been hit in the face. He straightened, recovering from surprise and shock enough to admire the girl's figure, but she didn't give him much time to continue his admiration. She ran to the bureau and picked up a small revolver. She spun around to face him, the hammer back.

Klein didn't hesitate, he had doubted that her father would shoot, but he had no doubt about the girl. He jumped to one side and slammed the door shut.

"That bitch of a daughter of yours would have killed me," he said, his voice trembling.

"And no jury would have found her guilty of murder," Smith said. "She told me not to let you in. She was right."

Klein was tempted to risk the revolver in the girl's hand and go into the bedroom, but the temptation didn't last long.

Klein quickly crossed the room to the other door, Smith turning so that the shotgun was on him all the way. He opened the door and with one glance saw that this was Smith's room and that Barney's body

150

wasn't here.

"We'll have a look in the barn," Klein said. "Jay expects me to fetch the body back to Rainbow."

"You can take it if you can find it," Smith said. "Just get out of here and stay out."

Klein strode to the front door, then stopped, his hand on the knob. He said, "I figger we'll be back, Smith. You're in one hell of a fix, but you don't seem to know it. Jay's bound to have your hide. I can't hold him off much longer." Klein hesitated before going on. "But there is one way you can get out of this if you want to."

Smith wasn't sure if he wanted to know what was on Klein's mind, but decided to hear him out. "All right, what is it?"

"With Barney dead, I inherit Rainbow, and I've got no quarrel with you," Klein said. "As long as Jay's alive, I'll do what he says, but if he was out of the way, you'd have no more trouble with Rainbow. I won't make a move against you between now and dark. No one's in the house except Jay and his wife. He'll be sitting beside the window where he always is, watching you or trying to. If you show up before sundown, none of the crew will interfere with you."

"I'm supposed to shoot him?"

Klein nodded. "It's the only way. With Jay

making the threats he's been making, and with the evidence there is that he's off his rocker, no jury would call it anything but self-defense. You'd better start thinking about it because dark ain't far off."

Klein opened the door and left the house. He strode through the snow to the barn, Bean pacing behind him. A search of the barn turned up neither a body nor any sign that one had been there.

"Might as well get back to Rainbow," Klein said. "I sure don't know what Smith done with the body."

They mounted and rode toward Rainbow, Bean asking, "Think he'll try to get Jay?"

"Hell, no," Klein said.

He hadn't really thought when he'd answered Bean. There was no room in his mind for anything except the image of Ruth's soft, white body. He burst out, "Monte, I'm going to have that girl before I leave the country."

"Rick Proctor ain't gonna like it," Monte said.

Klein laughed shortly. "So?"

"So we'd better get rid of Rick," Bean said.

Klein nodded. "That's exactly what we'll do."

CHAPTER 15

Rick stood motionless in front of Mrs. Laird's house staring at Curly Klein's back as he rode away. "Your brother was shot and killed this afternoon by Milt Smith." The words raced through his mind like a chorus.

Klein was wrong. He had to be. Smith was not capable of killing a man, any man, unless it was to defend his life, or Ruth's. And Barney would never threaten Milt or Ruth under any circumstances.

Suddenly the rest of what Klein had said ran through Rick's mind, "You'd better get out to Rainbow." He strode into the house, dropped his books on the table, and called to Mrs. Laird not to wait supper for him.

He had no intention of going to Rainbow, and he wondered why Klein had even suggested it. He knew, and Klein certainly knew, that he could not say or do anything that would change his father's attitude toward Milt Smith. If he told Jay that he was going to marry Milt's daughter, he would make a crazy man even crazier. He'd better stay clear of Rainbow and Jay Proctor.

Rick charged into the sheriff's office, slammed the door, and stood against it for a moment, panting hard. The cold air hurt his lungs and made him cough. He stood there several moments struggling for breath before he could talk.

Osmand had been pacing back and forth more nervous than Rick had ever seen him. He asked, "You've heard?"

Rick nodded. "Klein stopped long enough to tell me." He studied Osmand, his breath coming easier now. "If you've heard, why ain't you on your way out to the Rafter S?"

Osmand sat down at his desk and wiped his face. Suddenly he looked like a very old man, his mouth sagging open, the lines around his eyes and down his cheeks deeper than they had been the last time Rick saw him. Or so they seemed. He appeared to be dead tired, but he probably had not left his office all day.

"Why?" he said bitterly. "All right, Rick, I'll tell you why. This has been a purty peaceful county ever since I pinned on the star, and that was a hell of a long time ago. I'm old and beat and I'm serving my last term as sheriff. I wouldn't have run this time if your pa hadn't talked me into it."

He swallowed and sucked in a long breath. "Now your pa's gone loco. He's hired a ramrod who's a damned scoundrel. We get the coldest day we've had for years, and we get a murder that don't make no sense. I can't believe that Milt Smith shot your brother and I ain't gonna arrest him for it on Klein's say so."

"Milt didn't shoot Barney," Rick said. "I know he didn't. That's why we've got to get out there and talk to Milt. You've got to arrest somebody, sheriff. You can't just let Barney's murder go and forget it."

Osmand sighed. "No, I reckon not, though I don't know what I can do. I don't know who to arrest. If I ride out there to the Rafter S in this weather, I'll get chilled and my rheumatism will kill me for weeks."

Anger began building in Rick. Rheumatism or not, this was Osmand's job, and there was no way out for him. He was close to saying that and more, but he saw Osmand reach for his coat, so he held his tongue.

Osmand slapped his hat on his head and buttoned up his sheepskin. "I don't know what I can do," he muttered. "But let's go find out."

Rick followed Osmand out the door and

fell into step beside him. They got their horses from the livery stable, saddled up, and rode through the archway. The instant they appeared in the street, a man called, "Sheriff, over here."

The stage had pulled up in front of the hotel. Rick wondered why it was here. Ordinarily the stage left in the morning and wasn't back until the following afternoon. Osmand reined toward the stage, muttering something under his breath. When he reached the stage, Jack Noble, the driver, came out of the hotel.

"I was just coming after you, sheriff," Noble said. "We were held up this morning by two masked men. They took Joe Hawks off the stage, but they didn't bother nobody else and didn't even ask for the strong-box. We went on, but we hadn't gone far until we heard some shots. I didn't want to turn back, figuring there wasn't anything I could do.

"Well, we got as far as Deadman's Canyon and we couldn't go no farther. You know how the snow drifts in there in a storm. We had a hell of a time turning around and getting out, but we finally made it. On the way back we stopped at the bridge over Frenchman Creek. That was where we was held up this morning. We found Hawks' body under the bridge with about a foot of snow on him. He'd been shot through the brisket. Twice." He shook his head, and added, "It was murder, sheriff. Cold-blooded murder. That's just what it was."

Osmand looked at Rick and grimaced. "One murder on a day like this ain't enough. We've got to have two." He turned his gaze back to the driver. "Who was this Joe Hawks? I don't know of anybody around here by that name."

Noble shrugged. "All I know is he's a cattle buyer. He came in on the stage yesterday and tried to leave today. Where he came from or why he was here is something I can't tell you. He didn't talk much."

"I know him," Rick said. "Pa's dealt with him for years. He's from Kit Carson. I never knew him to come here before. Usually he stays close to home. Pa always had to go there to see him."

Osmand turned back to the driver. "You know the men who took Hawks off the stage?"

Noble shook his head. "They wore masks, like I told you. I never got a glimpse of their faces. They were wearing heavy coats with the collars pulled up around their necks. Hell, they could have been anybody."

"What'd they look like?"

The driver shrugged. "Just two men. Cowboys, I reckon. One was medium tall. Well built. The other one was a regular high pockets. Like Long John Wheeler. I ain't saying it was him, mind you. Just built like him."

"See any tracks in the snow?"

The driver shook his head. "The wind had been blowing the snow around something fierce. Any tracks they would have made was covered by the time we got there."

Long John Wheeler was, along with Monte Bean, Klein's right-hand man. Rick saw no reason why Klein would want Hawks murdered, but there weren't many men in the county who were built like Long John Wheeler. The second man was probably Monte Bean.

Rick leaned forward in the saddle. "Jack, think about the short man. Forget about Rainbow and Curly Klein. Was he built like Monte Bean?"

The driver shuffled his feet and stared at the snow in front of him. "Well, yeah, he was built a little like Bean, but I ain't saying it was him, so don't you go telling your pa and Klein that I said it was Bean."

He was scared, and he had a right to be, Rick thought. He'd never testify as long as Klein and his men were riding high, but that might change. He said, "Jack, I told you to forget Klein and Rainbow and my pa. You've heard Bean's voice when he was in town Saturday nights, yelling and raising hell. Did that second man sound like Bean?"

Noble glanced up at Osmand and then at Rick. He swallowed and shuffled his feet again, then he said reluctantly, "Yeah, well, I reckon his voice did sound a little like Bean's, but I tell you I ain't going into court and swear it was Bean."

"That's who it was, sheriff," Rick said, "and you can count on Klein ordering the murder, but I don't know why."

"We'll find out," Osmand said. "Take the body over to Doc's place. I'll look at it later."

"Ain't you gonna look at it now?" the driver asked. "I tell you it was murder and them damned killers —"

"I'll look at the body later," Osmand said sharply. "Right now I've got another murder to look into."

He reined away from the stage and took the road to the Big Sandy, then turned upstream to Smith's Rafter S, Rick riding beside him.

Osmand said nothing until they were out of town, then he glanced at Rick. "Men don't get murdered without a reason. Klein's been giving the orders on Rainbow, and Barney's the kind of man who could be fooled. He'd do what Klein told him to, seeing as your pa made Klein foreman. Klein didn't know until today, or maybe yesterday, that he's next in line after Barney to inherit Rainbow. Let's say Klein has been holed up because he's wanted by the law and now he figures it's safe to move."

Rick nodded. "Only he ain't the kind of man to go without filling his pockets first, and Rainbow cattle could fill his pockets. Maybe he's already started to sell our beef to Joe Hawks."

"I was thinking along them lines," Osmand said thoughtfully, "but why did Hawks come to Proctor City, and why did Klein order him murdered after he did come and was trying to leave town? It would have been safer just to let him go."

Rick shook his head. "I dunno, unless Hawks was trying to blackmail him, and I don't think Hawks was that kind of man. He might have known something about Klein, like who he was before he came here."

"If he knew Klein that well," Osmand said, "he wouldn't risk it. No, there's something else, and maybe it's tied in with the rest of this business, of the will and Barney's killing and Rainbow going to Klein."

"Sheriff, if you leaned on Jack," Rick said,

"leaned real heavy, he'd start remembering that he did recognize the men who held the stage up."

"I figure he will," Osmand agreed. "If we put Klein where he belongs, Jack will remember without being leaned on. I ain't in no hurry, though. Right now I'm more anxious to find out who killed Barney." He paused, and added, "I wish your ma wasn't out there at Rainbow."

"So do I," Rick said. "Maybe we oughtta go after her today."

"Maybe," Osmand said.

From the tone of his voice, Rick knew he had no such intention. It probably wouldn't do any good if they did go. He had tried before to get her to leave his father, but she had obeyed Jay Proctor so long that it had become a habit, a habit so strong that her ability to make decisions by herself was destroyed.

Still, Rick continued to worry about his mother's safety. Two men had been murdered. Certainly Curly Klein would not stop at murdering a woman if she was in his way.

CHAPTER 16

Mary Proctor sat in her rocking chair beside the kitchen window. Her gaze wandered over the woodshed, the pile of wood that was now a round mound of snow, the privy, and the apple tree, totally naked of leaves. She thought how Barney and Rick had played under that tree, had climbed it and fallen out of it. She looked at the biggest limb that the boys had used to chin themselves on, and suddenly the tears began to flow.

She wiped her eyes with a handkerchief that was already wet. She remembered how cuddly Barney had been when he was a baby, how slow he had been to walk, how long it had taken to wean him. He had grown up into a mild and gentle man, too mild for a father like Jay Proctor, too mild to stand up to a man like Curly Klein. Maybe that very gentleness that she had loved so much in him had been responsible for his death. Maybe he should have fought when he didn't.

No, Jay Proctor was the cause of Barney's death, no two ways about it. Jay had sent him to warn Milt Smith that he had only twenty-four hours to leave his home. Milt had been a good neighbor. He had never seemed like a violent man to her, but even a slow-tempered man could be pushed into violence, and Milt Smith had been pushed very hard. She could not blame him. He had not accomplished anything by shooting Barney, but he must have thought he might.

She was sure of only one thing. Jay Proctor had let his greed and ambition and self-pity drive him crazy and that had been the cause of Barney's death. She rose, fed the range with wood, and noticed that the box was nearly empty. She put her coat on and left the house, rebelling when she thought how many men were around the ranch doing nothing, or idly playing poker in the bunk-house. She knocked snow from a dozen sticks of stove wood and carried them into the kitchen and dropped them into the box behind the range.

She made herself a cup of tea and returned to the rocker. She sat there rocking and drinking the hot tea, the lump in her throat so big she could hardly swallow. Her gaze was on the rolling hills to the north that were blanketed by the glistening snow. The wind had been tossing the snow around like feathers, but now it had died down and everything seemed strangely still.

Suddenly Jay shouted from the front room, "Bring me a cup of coffee."

She hesitated, her bitterness toward Jay taking hold of her. She considered just sitting and pretending she didn't hear, but she knew he would continue to yell at her. She rose, poured the coffee, and carried it to him, hating herself because she was doing what he asked. He deserved nothing from her, absolutely nothing.

She handed the cup to him, noticing the revolver on his lap. He was capable of any act of violence as long as he had the gun. She was tempted to snatch it from him, but she wasn't sure she could move fast enough, and she was afraid of what would happen if she failed.

"Send for Rick," she said. "I want him here."

"No," Jay said. "I never want to see him again."

"He's the only son you have," she said.

He glared at her over the rim of his coffee cup. "He's no son of mine," he snapped. "Don't try to ram him down my throat. He knows how I feel. He deserted me when I needed him. Now, by God, he can just stay away."

"You can't let this new will stand, Jay," she cried. "Now that Barney's gone, you've got to change it. We've put most of our lives into Rainbow. You can't give it to a man like Curly Klein."

"You think Rick's gonna get Rainbow?" he demanded. "Oh, no. Curly is more of a son to me than Rick. The will stays just the way it is."

She stared at him, her hate for him a fever in her. A vision — she did not know what else to call it — raced through her mind. She would kill him. She turned away and walked into the bedroom, opened the drawer of the bureau that held the gun, and for a long moment stared at the little revolver.

She had been dominated so long by Jay Proctor that she did not think she could ever use the gun to kill him. But still the picture was in her mind: of holding the gun, pulling back the hammer, squeezing the trigger, hearing the sharp little crack, and then watching Jay's head tip forward on his chest.

She had seen this in her mind before, but never quite as clearly as now. She should do it now before anything else happened that was violent and evil. But she could not. She closed the drawer and turned away, telling herself that nothing was powerful enough to force her to fulfill this vision, but she had seen so many of her visions turn into reality that she could not dismiss this one lightly.

She lay down on her cot and closed her eyes, and again the tears came. It seemed such a short time ago that she had held Barney in her arms and nursed him; a short time ago when he had been a helpless baby dependent on her. She had sensed when he had left Rainbow this morning that she would never see him alive again, but there had been nothing she could do to stop him. Just as there had been nothing she could do when Rick had made his final break with Jay and had left Rainbow.

She had not intended to, but she dropped off to sleep. When she woke, she was so tired she wasn't even sure she was alive. She couldn't move. All she could do was to lie there and realize that she had a mind that was alive whether her body was or not. Men's voices broke into her consciousness.

At first she could not make out the words, then she was sure one voice was Jay's, the other Curly Klein's. This brought her fully awake with the hope that Klein knew more about Barney's death than he had known earlier in the day when he had first brought word of the shooting. Perhaps Barney was even alive, although she realized that was a forlorn hope.

"All right, I made a mistake," Klein was saying hotly, raising his voice so that Mary heard every word. "I should have picked Barney's body up when I first seen it. I could have roped it across my saddle and led my horse. But I thought I ought to notify you, so I came back to Rainbow in a hurry, then I sent Monte and Long John after it. I rode to town then, figuring I ought to notify Rick and the sheriff."

"It don't make no never mind about Rick," Jay shouted, "but I suppose Osmand had to know. What I want is for the body to be here where it belongs."

"Who'd ever think Smith would hide it?" Klein demanded, his voice lower than it had been, but still loud enough for Mary to hear what he said. "Besides, it was less'n a hundred yards from the Smith house. I figgered that if Smith was mean enough to plug Barney, he'd do the same with me if I got that close."

"Yeah, maybe he would have," Jay admitted, "but it still don't make any sense that Smith would hide it. Why?"

"I sure don't know," Klein said. "I tell you, I searched the house. Milt had his shotgun on me all the time, but he didn't keep me from looking. It seemed like he knew damned well I wouldn't find anything. There's just four rooms in the house. He didn't have no place to hide the body. We even moved the hay in the mow, figuring he might have covered Barney with it, but I tell you there just wasn't" — he stopped suddenly, as if thinking of something he had missed, then went on quickly — "a body there."

Jay was silent for a few seconds, then said angrily, "All right, get the crew together and go back. Burn him out. Take along enough powder to blow their house to hellangone. I don't care what you do. Just see that Milt Smith is dead."

"I don't like it," Klein said. "It ain't necessary. For one thing, the law will take care of Smith. Osmand can't shut his eyes to a killing like this. For another thing, that house is like a fort. You've heard Milt say he built it for a fort against the Indians. We can't burn him out in this weather, and we can't get close enough to blow it up without getting our tails shot off."

"By God, Curly," Jay said in exasperation, "I never knowed you to be scared of anything before."

"I ain't scared," Klein snapped. "I reckon what sticks in my craw is that there's a girl in Smith's house, and if we do something like blowing it up, she'll get killed along with Smith. I don't cotton to killing women, no matter what their pa's done."

"I don't care nothing about the girl," Jay bellowed. "You're looking for excuses. It's her bad luck that she's sticking with Smith. She can go to town and be safe. I've sent 'em a warning. That's why Barney's dead. Now you're asking me to go easy because a girl's in the house."

"The law —" Klein began.

"To hell with the law," Jay broke in. "You think Osmand will do anything if I'm not on his tail."

"Then get on his tail."

"No, we'll stomp our own snakes," Jay snapped. "If I could get out of this damned chair, I'd do it myself. Don't think for a minute that I can't change my will again if you ain't gonna carry out my orders."

Silence seemed to run on and on. Mary wished she could see Klein's face. She knew he'd be furious and fighting to control his temper, that a man as proud and strong-minded as he was would be outraged when Jay threatened him like that.

Presently Klein said, "All right, Jay, but it'll have to be after dark. I promised Smith he had until then."

"No, no," Jay yelled in a frantic voice. "Do it now."

Silence again. Then Klein said coldly, "Jay, you can threaten me about changing your will till hell cools off, but there's some things, like when and how, you've got to let me decide. If you can't do that, just roll your chair down there to Smith's place and take care of him yourself."

She heard Klein's boot heels crack against the floor; she heard the door slam, and then silence once more. She didn't move. For a moment she had hoped Klein would turn on Jay. She'd thought he was going to, but he had controlled himself better than she had expected.

Then, and the thought was like a knife thrust into her belly, she remembered that, with Barney gone, only Jay stood between Curly Klein and Rainbow. She was certain that he was a man who would murder Jay to get the ranch, and if she was here to see it, he would have to murder her, too.

She broke out into a cold sweat. She had not thought of this before, but now she wondered why she hadn't. She had sensed from the first that Klein was capable of any act of violence or treachery, an insight that Jay had not shared even in his saner moments. He didn't now.

But how could she leave? She realized then that even if she had a way to leave Rainbow, she probably wouldn't. As much as she hated Jay, she could not bring herself to go off and leave him. There simply was no one else who would look after him. No, she could not do that even to an animal.

"I want my supper," Jay yelled.

"All right, Jay," she called.

She rose and for a moment stood in front of her bureau mirror staring at her reflection. She was shocked by how old she looked, years older than her actual age. She could thank Jay for that, she thought bitterly. It had been a long time since she had given thought to how she looked. Now, she didn't really care whether she died today or not.

She took her hair down and brushed it and carefully braided it and pinned it back again. Once more Jay shouted, "I want my supper, Mary. What the hell are you doing?"

"I'm coming," she said.

She left the bedroom, pausing for a time in the front room to stare at the back of Jay's head and shoulders just visible above his chair. The neck and shoulders were as strong and muscular as ever. There had been a time when she had been proud of his strength, a time when he had been a decent human being capable of love and compassion.

Well, he wasn't capable of anything now except hate and an insatiable greed that demanded more and more. Staring at him and noting how motionless he sat, she told herself that he was made of stone, carved out of granite without a decent human thought or emotion.

Turning, she went into the kitchen, built up the fire, and started supper.

CHAPTER 17

Rick and the sheriff were half a mile or so from the Smith house when they came up on the rig ahead of them. The driver was hunkered down in the snow in front of his horse, apparently studying something in front of him. He rose, brushed snow from his overcoat, and stepped back into the buggy.

The sheriff saw the rig, too. He asked, "Now who do you suppose that is?"

Rick didn't answer. He had no more idea of the man's identity than Osmand had. It wouldn't be Klein or one of the Rainbow riders. For just a moment he wondered if his mother had hooked up the buggy and had come to see Barney's body, but he dismissed the thought immediately. Then he recognized the horse. It was Doc Doan's.

"It's Doc, sheriff," Rick said. "Why would he be out here on a day like this? If Barney's dead —"

"Milt might be sick," Osmand interrupted. "Or Ruth."

He was probably right, Rick thought. Still, the possibility that Barney might be alive and Ruth or Smith had gone to town for the doctor was a thought that haunted him. A wild hope, he told himself, because Klein had said definitely that Barney was dead.

Doan waited for them, sitting slack in the seat, the lines in his right hand. Before Rick reached him, he called, "What fetched you out here today, Doc?"

"Kind of cold for old men like us to be out, ain't it, sheriff?" Doan asked, ignoring Rick's question.

"Sure is," Osmand answered. "My rheumatiz is gonna give me hell tomorrow."

"Doc, I asked you what brought you out here today," Rick demanded.

Still Doan didn't answer the question. Instead, he pointed to the ground. "Milt told me about where Barney had been shot, so I drove along slow and found it. Looks to me like the bushwhacker hid yonder." He gestured with a hand. "Hard to tell because the snow's moved around some, but it was protected from the wind here. You can see Barney's blood. See that red snow right there?"

He pointed again, this time to where he

had been squatting in the snow. "I'd say he fell off his horse about there and tried to crawl. Chances are he knew that if he didn't get back to Smith's, he'd die right here in the road. You can see where he dragged himself through the snow a piece, but he must have lost consciousness before he went very far. Milt and Ruth heard the shots, hitched up a wagon, and hauled him back to the house within a few minutes from the time he'd been hit. Lucky for him that they picked him up so soon."

"Then he's alive?" Rick asked, exasperated at the way Doan kept refusing to answer his question.

Doan glanced at Rick, then at Osmand. "I dunno if he's alive right now or not," he said reluctantly. "Klein was here a while ago with Monte Bean. They rousted Milt and Ruth around some, though they left me alone. They looked all over for Barney, but they didn't find him. I ain't one to tell you your job, sheriff, but you could bring Klein in for trespassing, I reckon, or threatening Milt and the girl. He sure got out of line."

"Damn it, Doc, you still ain't telling me much," Rick said. "You're saying Barney was alive when you left the house?"

"Yeah, he was alive then," Doan said. "Now I'll tell you a thing or two I can't prove. I figure Klein was the one who shot Barney. He must have figured Barney was dead or he wouldn't have ridden off and left him. Of course he didn't want to show himself to the Smiths, so he didn't get a close look at Barney. I don't know what chance he has, Rick. He's got a good nurse and if she keeps him warm, I'd say . . ."

Rick didn't wait to hear the rest of what Doc had to say, but dug in the steel and roared past him, snow flying behind his horse. He pulled up in front of the house and, leaving the reins dragging, ran to the porch and pounded on the door.

Smith must have seen him coming because he opened the door immediately, saying, "Come in, boy. Ruth's with Barney in the bedroom."

Rick knocked snow from his boots and strode across the front room to the bedroom door. Ruth was sitting beside the bed. She turned when she heard his steps, cried out when she saw who it was, and ran to him.

"Rick, Rick," she said, and threw her arms around him and hugged him. "I don't know what to do. I just sit here and look at him and feel so helpless."

Rick stared past her at Barney, who lay on his back. He couldn't tell whether his brother was breathing or not. He looked like a dead man, the skin of his face gray, his eyes closed, his pale lips slightly parted.

"He's alive?"

"Oh, he's alive," she said, "but I don't know how long he'll be alive. The doctor said there wasn't anything now we could do but keep him warm and wait." She turned from Rick, slipped a hand under the covers, and shook her head. "I'll get some hot irons. It doesn't take long for them to cool."

She ran out of the room. Rick sat down, the snow that still clung to his boots melting and making puddles on the floor. He didn't notice. He still found it hard to believe that this was Barney. He could see now that his brother was breathing, his chest rising and falling slowly and regularly. But Barney's face was so pale and drawn, his cheeks sunken, that there was little resemblance between him and the brother Rick had known.

Ruth ran back into the bedroom, holding two hot irons wrapped in thick folds of newspaper. She slipped one under the covers on one side, then did the same on the other side of the bed, removing the cool irons as she slipped the hot ones into place.

"I'll put these irons back on the stove," she said.

She returned a moment later and stood

beside Rick, one arm over his shoulders. She said in a low tone, "It's so hard just to sit beside his bed and watch him and know there's nothing I can do but wait. The doctor said he had a good chance to pull through, but I don't know. He's hardly opened his eyes or moved since we brought him in and put him into bed."

Rick heard voices from the front room and knew that the sheriff had come in.

Presently Smith called, "Ruth. Rick. Come here. We want to talk to you."

Rick glanced at Ruth, wondering what there was to talk about.

Ruth nodded. "We can sit out there as well as here. I'll come back in a little while and see about the irons. The doctor said he mustn't chill. Pa built a fire in the heater so the room's pretty warm. He hated to use the wood because he doesn't have much in the house and he's afraid to go outside, but he had to get the bedroom warm."

"Why is he afraid to go outside?" Rick asked.

"I guess that's what he wants to talk to you about," Ruth said.

Rick followed her into the front room, puzzled. Smith was on one side of the heater, the sheriff on the other, his hands extended over the stove. Smith motioned toward a chair and Rick sat down, taking time to look at the man. He was shocked by what he saw.

To Rick, Milt Smith had always been a strong, square-jawed man who could be depended on to hold his own in any kind of trouble. Now Rick was seeing a frightened stranger, pale-faced, sweating, his hands trembling as he took a bandanna out of his pocket and wiped his forehead.

He looked at Rick and nodded. "I know what you're thinking, son, but I've got just one question. Were you ever scared? I mean, really scared right down into the bottom of your guts till you were sick?"

"No," Rick admitted. "I was never that scared. Maybe I'm not smart enough to be scared."

"I don't know as to that," Smith said, "but I guess a man thinks less about such things when he's younger. I've been worried about Ruth, too. When you were here last night I was talking tough as nails. Well, I'm not that tough now. I wish I'd sold out to Jay when he started putting the pressure on me, but I reckon it's too late now."

"What happened?" Rick asked. "Doc said that Klein and Bean were here."

Smith nodded. "That's it. I never gave this business much thought until they showed up. I guess I kept thinking that Jay was really bluffing and I'd just bluff back, but after hearing what Klein had to say, I know it's no bluff. He'd have killed Barney for sure if he'd found him."

"I don't see how you hid him," Rick said.

"That's part of the story," Smith said. "They showed up and Ruth said not to let 'em in. I reckon she was right, but I didn't do it. I didn't want to hear Klein hammering on the door and yelling at me." He shrugged. "No, that wasn't it. I wanted to hear what he had to say. I mean, I kept hoping that Jay didn't really mean all of his threats I've been hearing. Fact is, I didn't want to believe 'em.

"Anyway, before I let 'em in, Ruth ran into the bedroom and shut the door. I didn't know what she was up to. They came in and Klein looked into the kitchen and saw Doc sitting there by the stove. He wanted to know what Doc was doing here and I told him my heart was kicking up and I guess he believed me."

Smith swallowed and wiped his face again. "Rick, I had my shotgun on that bastard all the time he was here. It's hell to discover that your sand's all run out. I didn't believe it before. I could have blowed him in two any time. I've never shot a man. I've never even shot at a man, but I always thought I could if I had to. Well, I found out I couldn't. If Klein had threatened Ruth, I — I don't know if I could have or not."

"Don't forget Monte Bean was out here with you all that time," Ruth said.

"Sure, it meant I'd have got plugged, but by God, I should have blowed Klein's head off anyway and taken a chance with Bean. Of course it never came to a showdown, but I just don't know what I'd have done if it had. One thing I didn't figure on was Ruth showing herself to that son-of-a-bitch as naked as a jay bird."

"What?" Rick shouted. "What are you talking about?"

"It was my idea," Ruth said. "I knew I had to keep Klein from finding Barney, and we didn't have any place to hide him. All I could figure out was to fix it so he'd look right at Barney and not see him. I thought that if I shocked him enough, he'd back out without really looking. So I took off all my clothes and piled them and everything else I had on top of the bed so it looked like I'd just done a big washing and was folding my clothes. From the doorway he couldn't see the bulge that Barney made under the covers."

She giggled nervously, glancing at Rick,

and then turning her gaze away. "I guess he didn't expect to see a naked woman. It stopped him right there in the doorway which was what I was counting on. I cussed him and threw my boot at him and ran over to the bureau and got my gun. He backed out of the room in a hurry and told pa that his bitch of a daughter would have shot him. I would have, too, if he'd come on into the room."

"You took one hell of a chance, it seems to me," Rick said. He paused and then added, "I guess Curly Klein has seen more of you than I have."

They laughed, breaking the tension. "You'll see the same on the night we're married and that's going to be soon. I've done some hard thinking, Rick. I — I, well, I just don't want to put it off any longer."

"I'm glad to hear that," Rick said, "but it may be too late."

"I don't think so," Osmand said. "I guess I'm like Milt. I don't cotton to getting killed, and I don't know what I'd do till I face a deal like this. I've been standing here listening and I'm beginning to hate myself. I've been partly to blame for what's happened. I should have gone out to Rainbow and told Jay what to expect from me as soon as I heard what was going on, but I kept making excuses about being an old man and my rheumatiz and the cold weather."

Rick rose, his gaze on the lawman. "I don't see that anything's changed, sheriff."

Osmand shrugged. "All right, I'm still an old man and the weather is too cold to be out in and my rheumatiz is gonna kill me tomorrow, but I'm riding to Rainbow. It may be too late, but I'm going anyway."

"Then you'd better go before dark," Smith said.

"Why?" Osmand asked.

"Klein gave me a chance to solve all our problems," Smith said. "I'm supposed to go to Rainbow and shoot Jay. He promised not to make a move before dark. I reckon he'd do the same for you."

Rick stared at the sheriff thoughtfully, wondering what had changed the lawman's mind. Ruth was the one who had showed real courage. She had saved Barney and postponed a bloodbath. Maybe just having heard about it had given Osmand this attack of bravery.

"I'll go with you, sheriff," Rick said. "Maybe we won't do any good, but it's worth a try."

CHAPTER 18

For a moment the others stared at Rick as if shocked by what he'd said, then Smith shook his head. "I don't think you ought to. They won't likely bother the sheriff, seeing as he's a county official who can claim he's there on county business, but Klein probably figures you're as dangerous to him as Barney was. You're the one who can take Jay's will into court."

"I'd like for you to stay here," Ruth said. "I'd feel safer."

Rick glanced at Osmand, not sure that the sheriff welcomed his company. "No, I'm going. I want to see ma." He nodded at Smith. "Milt, let's go fetch in enough wood to go through the night. Ruth can't keep Barney warm if we don't keep enough wood in the house for a good fire."

Smith hesitated, then shrugged his shoulders as if thinking it wasn't worth an argument. Both men put on their coats and went out through the back door, Smith making a quick survey of the yard before he stepped off the porch.

The wind had not picked up, and the snow lay on the ground like a motionless blanket, the late afternoon sun throwing the men's long shadows beside them as they strode to the woodpile.

"I'll split," Rick said. "You carry."

They worked hard for fifteen minutes or more, Rick splitting the wood as fast as Smith could carry it into the kitchen and pile it along the wall. Presently Smith said, "That's enough for the range. We'd better take some big chunks in for the heater. I didn't figure on this cold snap. It's gonna be nip and tuck if we make it into summer on the wood I've got. Last fall I thought we had plenty."

Three trips were enough to pile up all the wood the heater would use during the night. Rick called from the kitchen doorway, "I'll walk around to the front, sheriff. No use making tracks across Ruth's clean floor."

"I'll have supper ready when you get back," Ruth said as Rick closed the door and strode around the house to the front, his boots crunching in the snow.

Osmand came out through the front door as Rick mounted. The sheriff said, "Sure you want to do this?"

"I'm sure," Rick answered. "Like I told you, I'm worried about ma. Chances are I can't get her to leave, but I'll try. I feel guilty for not going sooner." He paused, then added, "I've got to face pa sometime. I might just as well get it over with."

Osmand pulled himself into the saddle, grunting with the effort. He muttered, "Damned if I won't be glad when my term's over."

They took the road that led downstream, then turned and crossed the bridge and pointed their horses toward Rainbow.

Rick said, "I reckon pa can see us now. I guess he don't do nothing all day but sit at the window and watch what's going on."

"Won't take him long to recognize us," Osmand said.

Rick guessed that the sheriff was thinking that Jay might cut loose as soon as they were in range. He realized it was a possibility, though he didn't think Jay had gone that far downhill mentally. Rick had no doubt in his mind about Jay Proctor being insane, but there were degrees of insanity, and Jay was still coherent enough to give orders to Klein and go through the motions of running a cattle ranch.

Still, Rick had not been home for so long

that he really *didn't* know how far gone his father was. Luckily, nothing happened as they approached the house, and each passing second gave him hope that nothing would. No one was in sight. Rainbow might as well have been deserted as far as any activity was concerned. The wind earlier in the day had blown the snow enough to cover most of the tracks that had been made that morning and early afternoon.

They dismounted in front of the house and tied, Rick's gaze sweeping the corrals and barns and bunkhouse. Smoke was pouring from the chimney of the bunkhouse and both chimneys of the ranch house. Rick felt a prickle ravel down his spine that was not from the cold. Along with the danger that Jay might go berserk was the distinct possibility that Klein would never let them reach the front door of the house.

Rick said nothing about his worries. Osmand had plenty of his own. He didn't hurry his steps, knowing he could not afford to show the slightest hint of fear, but he found it harder to keep the slow and steady pace with each step. He felt his skin crawl as he anticipated a slug slamming into his body; his ears strained for the crack of a Winchester from the bunkhouse.

He reached the porch and crossed it to

the front door. He gripped the knob and turned it. Opening the door, he went into the house, Osmand a step behind him. It was not until he felt the warm air of the room and heard Osmand close the door that he was able to draw a full breath.

Jay was sitting in his wheelchair staring out the window. He gave no sign that he knew anyone had come in.

Rick said, "Howdy, pa."

Still Jay ignored him. He sat motionless at the window, his gun across his lap, his gaze on the snow-covered slope below the house. Rick's mother was in the kitchen. The instant she heard his voice, she dropped what she was doing and ran into the front room.

"Rick," she cried. "I've been hoping you would come."

She ran to him and hugged him. Then, with her face against his shirt, she began to cry. Rick stood motionless, an arm around his mother, his gaze on his father. He had not been here for months, but he saw little change. The air in the big room crackled with hostility, and Rick marveled at his father's strength and will. Without saying a word or making a motion of any kind, he contrived to show Rick he hated him and did not want him here.

Osmand remained behind Rick for a time, his gaze moving from Jay to Rick and his mother, and back to Jay. Finally he crossed the room to stand beside Jay, asking, "How are you feeling?"

"Terrible," Jay said bitterly. "I'm a ~~god~~-damn prisoner in this chair. I've lost my only son and I can't do nothing to get the killer. I've always been a man to stomp my own snakes, but I can't do it now. I've got to depend on someone else."

"You're thinking that Milt Smith shot Barney?" Osmand asked.

"Of course that's what I'm thinking," Jay snapped. "I sent Barney to Smith's place to tell him he had twenty-four hours to sell and get out. He got sore and plugged Barney after he left the house. Then the son-of-a-bitch hid the body. Curly saw Barney lying in the road, but when he sent two men to bring him back, Barney was gone. Curly went to Smith's house looking for Barney, but he couldn't find him. Now you tell me what else there is to think."

Rick was afraid that Osmand was going to say Barney was still alive, but the sheriff didn't. He was silent for a moment, then he said slowly, "Jay, this ain't what you want to hear, but I'm going to say it anyway. I don't think Milt shot Barney. After you made your last will, you gave Klein plenty of reason to want Barney dead, and maybe even reason to see you dead."

Jay's head snapped around, and he stared at Osmond. This was the first chance Rick had to see his father's face. He was shocked. He had seen him change after his accident, but when he'd left home, Jay had been a reasonably sane man. Sure, he'd been given to temper fits when he'd said and done irrational things, but now he looked like a stranger.

Jay's face was thinner than Rick had remembered it, his skin hanging loosely under his jaws. His color was bad, almost the pallor of death, and his eyes were bloodshot and wild. Rick remembered seeing a man in town a couple of years before, a man who had gone berserk and had killed his wife. Jay had the same expression, and whatever slender hope Rick still nursed that his father could be reasoned with was gone.

Now Jay's face turned red. He stammered incoherently for a few seconds before he bellowed, "Why, you lying son-of-a-bitch! Curly is the nearest thing to a son I've got. He wouldn't shoot Barney." He jerked a thumb at Rick. "He might, but Curly wouldn't." He took a long breath, and asked, "Why ain't you in town in your warm office instead of gallivanting around in this weather?"

"I wish I was in town in my warm office," Osmand said grimly, "but I should have ridden out here before this. You can think what you want to about Klein. What I came out to tell you is that I've heard you've been talking about the law being Proctor law, that you wouldn't be touched no matter what you did. You're dead wrong, Jay. I know you helped me get elected, and maybe I've been guilty of looking the other way a few times when you done some capers that wasn't entirely legal, but I want you to get it through your stubborn head that murder is more'n I can stomach. If you carry out your threat to kill Milt Smith, I'll throw you in the jug as sure as your name is Jay Proctor."

Jay laughed, an unpleasant sound that sent chills racing down Rick's back. He could remember a time when his father had been able to laugh as well as the next man, but this was different, a strange, contemptuous sound that held no trace of humor.

"You're an old man, Osmand," Jay said, turning his head again to look through the window. "Don't try to pretend you're still young and full of piss and vinegar. You ain't."

Osmand turned away. "It's no use," he

said to Rick. "I've had my say. It ain't my fault if he won't listen."

Rick stepped away from his mother and walked toward Jay. He said, "Pa, Ruth's in the house with Milt. I'll be there, too. If you send Klein and his men down there, we'll have a fight. Ruth might get killed. So could I."

"Makes me no never mind," Jay said coldly.

Rick's mother tugged at his arm. "Come into the kitchen," she whispered, and motioned for Osmand to do the same. Leading the way, she walked into the kitchen and waited until both men had followed, then closed the door.

"I've started supper," she said. "I've got enough for both of you if you'll stay."

Rick shook his head. "I've got to get back. Ruth said she'd have supper ready. I didn't figure there was any use to come here tonight, but the sheriff wanted to talk to pa, and I thought I'd come along, mostly to see if you'd leave with me. You can stay at Smith's, or you can go to town and live with Mrs. Laird. Whatever you do, you've got to get away from here." He nodded toward the front room. "Pa's capable of anything."

"I know," she said dully. "Anything. I'm

ashamed to say it, Rick, but I wish he was dead."

Rick was not shocked to hear her say that. He had hoped for the same thing many times. Some people lived too long. If Jay would simply lie down and die, the situation would become a lot less complicated. But a great deal also depended on whether Barney lived or died. For a moment Rick considered telling his mother that Barney was alive, then decided against it. He still might die, and knowing that he wasn't dead at this particular moment would only give her false hope.

"We've got to go, ma," Rick said finally. "Put on your coat and go with us. You ain't safe here."

She shook her head. "I've thought about it a lot, Rick. I even considered leaving earlier today. I know I'm not safe here, but no matter how much I hate him and want to see him dead, this is my home. I just can't go off and leave."

Rick nodded, thinking this was exactly what he had expected her to say. He asked, "You've still got your gun?"

"Oh, yes," she said. "It's in my bureau drawer, but I'm going to get it and keep it with me. I don't know when I might need it."

"We've got to ride, ma," Rick said. "No use staying here any longer. I thought this was the way it would turn out, but we had to try. If it ends up that Klein takes his men to Smith's place and tries to kill us, we'll have to fight."

"It ain't gonna come to that," Osmand said. "I'm going to the bunkhouse and arrest Monte Bean and Long John Wheeler for the murder of Joe Hawks. I don't have much evidence right now, but I'll get it. Like you said, Jack Noble's memory will improve if I lean on him, and I'm getting so damned tired of this business that I'm going to lean hard."

"You're just trimming off the limbs," Rick said. "Nothing is gonna be settled till we get Klein."

"I'll take him in, too," Osmand said, "if he's here. That'll clip Jay's claws for him."

Rick could only shake his head. "Klein won't let you take him. You're just asking for a slug in your brisket, sheriff. I thought we rode up here to see what we could do with pa."

"That's right," Osmand said grimly. "I should have stayed in my warm office like Jay said and forgot all about my so-called duty. But I didn't, and now that I'm in this up to my neck, I've got to do what a sheriff is supposed to do." He sucked in a long breath and expelled it with a gusty sound. "I can stand some help, Rick."

Osmand was scared, and a scared man could be a dangerous man. If Osmand went into the bunkhouse alone, he'd get himself killed, and Rick could not afford that. Osmand might be weak and inept and a lot of other things, but he was the only lawman in the county. And he wasn't giving Rick any choice.

"I think you're wrong to tackle this," Rick said, "but if you're bound to go ahead, I'll back you up."

"Good," Osmand gave him a wry grin. "When I left the office this afternoon, I never thought I'd be into this."

"Neither did I," Rick said.

They went out through the back door, Rick glancing briefly at his mother. She was watching him intently as if she thought she would never see him again. Chances were she wouldn't.

CHAPTER 19

Curly Klein stood beside a bunkhouse window staring at the snow-covered yard that glittered brightly in the late afternoon sunshine. He rolled a cigarette, fired it, and drew on it, but he found no satisfaction in the taste. At this moment he couldn't find satisfaction in anything.

Five of the crew were sitting at a table near the stove playing poker. The rest were scattered around the room, some sprawled on their bunks, some working on their gear. The separation between the old hands and the new ones Klein had hired was more distinct than ever.

Klein had intended to lead them to the Smith place and lay siege to it just to satisfy Jay, but now he decided not to. The old hands wouldn't go. He hadn't forced them into a corner where they would refuse him, and he had no intention of doing so. Of course he couldn't be sure they would refuse to go, but he had a feeling it would work out that way. He'd led men of all kinds in all types of situations over the years. He had learned to sense things like this, and he had seldom been wrong.

There had been ten men in the Rainbow crew. Scott Shell was dead. Four were old hands. That left five to go with him if he decided to tackle the Smith place. That wasn't enough, not for a difficult job he didn't want to do in the first place. Besides, if he was going to kill Jay, which he would do once he was rid of Rick, there was no point in doing anything to satisfy the old man.

His course was clear. Get Rick up here, shoot him, then beef Jay and blame Rick for Jay's killing. He could admit that he had killed Rick himself, and Osmand wouldn't hold him. He'd claim self-defense, and some of his men would swear that his story was right. In one way it would be better if the old hands quit than if he fired them.

He always returned in his thinking to his basic problem. How did he get Rick to come to Rainbow? He tossed his cigarette stub to the floor and ground it out. He wasn't thinking straight. The trouble was that the mental image of Ruth Smith's naked body kept returning to him and blocking his thinking process.

Now that he'd had time to consider it, he was positive he had made a mistake in his judgment of Ruth. The girl was begging to be raped. He'd been a fool to back down from her bluff. A man didn't get many chances like that, and when he did, he'd best take it.

Suddenly Klein was aware that two riders were coming up the road. He forgot all about Ruth because one of them looked like Rick Proctor. But he wasn't alone, and Klein had to have Rick by himself if his scheme was to work. Maybe the other man was Milt Smith. If that was the case, it would still work out because Jay would certainly shoot Smith on sight.

"Monte," Klein called. "Come here."

Monte Bean got up from his bunk and crossed the room to the window. Klein asked, "Know either one of those men?"

Bean squinted, rubbed his eyes, and squinted some more. He muttered, "Damn if that sun ain't bright. Well, looks to me like the fellow on the right's Rick. I dunno about the other one, but he looks . . ." He stopped and sucked in a long breath. "Yeah, he sure does. Curly, the other one's the sheriff."

"No, he wouldn't be out in this kind of

weather." Klein said sharply. "That old booger's too lazy to get outside when he's got to . . ." He stopped and nodded. "No, by God, you're right. That's Osmand, but what would bring him out here?"

He wondered if by some crazy miracle the old sheriff had stumbled onto some proof that he was the one who had shot Barney. It couldn't be. But then it was against all logic that Osmand would be here with Rick.

Bean was uneasy, too. He said, "Maybe we oughtta brace 'em, Curly. Osmand may be after me for beefing Joe Hawks."

"No." Klein shook his head. "It ain't that I've got any love for that old goat. It's just that killing a man like Hawks or Barney ain't gonna get people all worked up, but you plug their sheriff and some of 'em will take it personal. We'd be into a hornet's nest. We've still got too much to do to stir up any more hell than we have to."

He watched Rick and Osmand tie, tramp through the snow to the front door, and go into the house. He muttered, "I'd like to see what Jay will do when he sees the kid. He hates Rick so much he may just shoot him on sight."

"You've got your shot at Rick now," Bean said. "I've got somethin to settle with him, too. I say let's take 'em when we've got a chance."

"No, damn it," Klein said sharply. "I told you we couldn't do it when Osmand's with him. We've got to get Rick when he's by himself. Maybe if we could make him think that Jay was making his will over again now that Barney's gone, he'd —"

"I'd feel better if we nailed Osmand, too," Bean said.

Klein wasn't listening. The thought of the will had given him the answer he'd been looking for. Judge Callahan did all Jay's legal work, and Rick would believe anything Callahan told him. He should have thought of it sooner.

"I'm riding into town," Klein said. "I don't figure that Rick will be here very long, but he'll be back before long and that's when we'll get him. You stay here and keep an eye on what happens. I don't think we'll have any problem. Osmand and Rick will pull out in a little while because they won't get anywhere with Jay."

"I dunno what business you've got in town," Bean said uneasily. "I'd feel better if you stayed here till Rick and the sheriff leave."

"What can an old goat like Osmand do?" Klein demanded.

"I dunno," Bean admitted, "but I'm about

ready to pull my freight. Don't seem to me that this deal is going like we planned, and with my record, I don't want Osmand arresting me for anything."

"It's going exactly like we planned," Klein snapped. "Don't get no ideas about running out on me or I'll hunt you down and put a window in your skull. I still need you and you sure as hell need me. I'll be back after supper."

He pulled on his sheepskin and slapped his hat on his head, glanced at the men who were paying no attention to him, and left the bunkhouse. Damn, it was cold, he told himself as he strode to the barn. It wasn't right to have this kind of weather so late in the year. When he got this deal wound up, he'd head back for Arizona. He should never have left.

He saddled his horse and rode around the back of the house, coming into the road just above the bridge. He was far enough from the house so he didn't think Jay or anyone there would see him. Or, if they did, he wouldn't be recognized at that distance.

When he reached town, he put his horse in the livery stable and told the hostler he'd be leaving again soon. He stepped into the street that was nearly deserted, wondering whether Callahan would still be in his office. The chances were he'd have gone before now. Klein wasn't familiar enough with the judge's habits to know what his schedule was, but he decided to try the office first just on the off chance he was still there.

He climbed the stairs and tried the knob. The door opened.

Callahan called, "I'm just leaving. I'll have to see you in the morning."

Klein stepped into the office and closed the door behind. "No, you'll see me now, judge."

Callahan was in the process of putting on a moth-eaten buffalo coat. He buttoned it, frowning. "I didn't know it was you, Curly. What brings you back to town?"

"I've got a question to ask," Klein said, "and then I'll tell you about a job you're going to do for me."

"Not tonight," Callahan said. "My wife will have supper ready when I get home. All I want to do is sit in front of the fire and smoke my pipe, and then go to bed. I haven't been warm all day. Now what's your question?"

"Suppose Jay kicks the bucket and Rick's still alive?" Klein said. "What are the chances that Rick or his mother or both could have the will set aside?"

"Pretty good," Callahan said. "They could argue that Jay made out his present will under duress, claiming that no man would make such a will if he was in right mind when he had a son and a wife still alive."

"But it'd take time, wouldn't it?" Klein asked. "And meanwhile I'd have Rainbow?"

"Oh, sure," Callahan said. "It would take time." He grinned. "You'd need a good lawyer, Curly, one who could swear that Jay was in his right mind and made this will without any hint of duress."

Klein nodded, wondering why he had ever thought he could stay here and run Rainbow. He guessed he felt the same as Monte Bean, that things weren't working out the way they had planned and it was safer to get out of the country. He would, too, as soon as he had gathered and sold the Rainbow cattle. That was like having money in the bank.

"All right," Klein said finally. "You're my lawyer and you're gonna do your first chore for me tonight. You're going to find Rick and tell him that his father wants to see him right away."

Callahan shook his head. "I don't have any idea where Rick is, and if you think I'm going sashaying around looking for him on a night like this —"

Klein grabbed him by the front of his coat and shook him until his teeth rattled. "Don't tell me what you won't do. It was your idea for me to salivate Jay and lay it onto Rick, and if this deal don't work out the way we're planning, that's exactly what I'll say. You're into this as much as I am, so don't try to weasel out of it."

Callahan's eyes narrowed. "What the hell are you talking about? All I said was that you needed a good lawyer —"

Klein slapped him across the side of the head. "You said it, all right. I know the kind of advice you gave me. Don't try to deny it. I reckon that if it got out that you were giving legal advice to commit murder, you'd be finished practicing law, wouldn't you?"

Callahan backed across the room until he ran into his desk. He stood cowering there, a badly frightened man. "What do you want out of me, Klein?" he asked, his voice trembling.

"That's better," Klein said. "You'll do what I tell you or I'll cut your heart out. Savvy?"

Callahan nodded.

Klein went on, "Rick was with the sheriff the last I saw him. That was at Rainbow this afternoon just before I came to town. If he ain't with Osmand, he'll be at the Smith place. You go home and eat your supper so Rick will have time to get to town or the Smith place. Then wait a little longer so there'll be time for a Rainbow rider to get Jay's message to you. You can tell Rick that Jay knew you wouldn't believe one of my men, but maybe he'll believe you."

Callahan shook his head. "It won't work. Rick's no fool. He won't believe it no matter who it comes from."

Klein thought about that a moment, then said, "All right, tell him you had to go to Rainbow to see Jay about some legal business and Jay told you to give Rick the message. That's logical. You'll have to wait long enough so there'd be time for you to ride to Rainbow and then go to Smith's place."

Klein moved to the door, then paused. "If you go home and get comfortable and eat your supper and go to sleep and forget the whole deal, you'll be going to sleep permanent-like."

Klein left the office, leaving a badly shaken lawyer staring at his back until he disappeared down the stairs. Callahan would do it, Klein told himself. The man was a sneaky shyster without a spoonful of guts in his entire body.

He paused at the foot of the stairs. It was almost dark, but he didn't want to meet Osmand or Rick on the road to Rainbow. He still thought they wouldn't stay long at Rainbow, but he wanted to give them plenty of time either to come on to town or make the turn to Milt Smith's place.

Not that he couldn't take care of himself if he met them on the road. It was just that they might get suspicious about why he was in town, and Rick would wonder if he had something to do with Callahan's message.

He wiped a hand across his face. Damn it, he was a doer. This scheming wasn't the kind of thing he did well. If the timing didn't work out, Rick would be suspicious. Better not take a chance on meeting Rick, he decided. He'd have supper in town, get a drink in the hotel bar, and then head back to Rainbow.

CHAPTER 20

Rick strode beside Osmand to the bunk-house, a sick cold feeling of dread settling in his belly. He could not understand why the old sheriff, who had been reluctant to do his job earlier in the day, was now so hell-bent on winding it up with a flourish.

"Why are we doing this?" Rick burst out.

Osmand shot him a quick glance. "Two reasons," he said. "Surprise is part of it. They ain't expecting us to make a move like this. The other is, I've got you to side me. Seeing as the county don't allow me a deputy, I figure I'd better make use of you while I can." He paused, then added, "Don't jump the gun, but keep your hand on the butt of your iron."

Osmand opened the door of the bunk-house and went in, Rick following. A wave of warm, tobacco-scented air struck them.

Someone yelled, "Shut the door."

Another said, "Born in a barn and raised

207

in a sawmill."

Rick slammed the door shut. In his first glance around the room he did not see Klein, but several of the men were lying on their bunks. The room was cloudy with tobacco smoke. It was possible Klein was here and Rick just didn't spot him.

Five men were sitting around the table in the middle of the room playing poker. Four were the old hands who had been riding for Rainbow since Rick had been a boy. The fifth was Long John Wheeler. Monte Bean was standing at a window. The other three Klein men were on their bunks.

Several of the men called, "Howdy, sheriff."

The four old Rainbow hands at the table greeted Rick warmly, but Klein's men acted like he wasn't even there. Wheeler was silent, his eyes whipping from Osmand to Rick and back to Osmand. It was plain the man was uneasy and nervous enough to be jumpy and therefore dangerous.

Monte Bean was the one who worried Rick. He moved to his left so he could watch both Bean and Wheeler, but he still didn't know how to play his hand. He couldn't take two men, and he wasn't sure that Osmand could get his gun out in time to do any good if it came to shooting.

"I'm arresting Wheeler and Bean for the murder of Joe Hawks," Osmand said. "Drop your gunbelts and —"

He never finished his sentence. The room simply exploded. Monte Bean went for his gun. Wheeler jumped out of his chair and tried for his gun, but two men sitting at the table were all over him, knocking him to the floor and wrestling the gun out of his hand.

Rick's right hand had been gripping the butt of his gun. He brought it up in a swift, rhythmical draw, cocking and firing at Monte Bean. He'd had no time to make a decision. It was simply that he considered Bean more dangerous than Wheeler, so he tried for him.

Bean was fast, faster than Rick, and he got off one shot. But he was in too much of a hurry. The slug slapped into the wall behind Rick.

Bean didn't fire a second time. Rick's slug caught him in the chest, knocking him back against the wall. He seemed to hang there a moment, his boot heels digging into the floor. Then they slid out from under him and he sprawled out full-length, his gun dropping from his hand.

Osmand had been struggling with his gun. Now he had it clear of leather and lined it on the Klein men in the back of the room.

He said, "You boys stand pat. I ain't after you, but if you try to take Wheeler from me, I'll run all three of you in."

Now Rick knew for sure that Klein was not here. It would have turned out differently if he had been. Two of the old hands were sitting on Wheeler. A third man, Slim Holman, said, "Don't worry about these yahoos, sheriff. They don't know enough to spit if Klein don't tell 'em to do it."

"Where is Klein?" Osmand asked.

"Dunno," Holman answered. "He was here a little while ago. He was standing there talking to Bean and then all of a sudden he was gone."

"Let him up." Osmand nodded at the men who were sitting on Wheeler. "We're beholden to you boys."

Rick couldn't remember when Slim Holman hadn't ridden for Rainbow. He was a grizzled, tobacco-chewing old cowhand who had been Rick's idol in his boyhood years. In those days Holman had been trusted by Jay, but now Jay had put his faith in Klein. Rick wondered why the old cowboy was still here.

Holman looked at Bean's body, then raised his gaze to Osmand. He said slowly, "We was glad to do it, sheriff. Rainbow has turned out to be a Goddamn nest of thieves and we've been looking for you to take a hand for a long time. We should have quit when Klein fired the others, but you get used to working for an outfit and we kept hoping Rick here would take hold. We figured Barney didn't have the guts to do the job."

Holman's gaze moved from Osmand to Rick. "How about it, boy? We can work for you, but if it's gonna go on being Klein, we're moving out."

"I'm taking over," Rick said. "I ain't real sure what to do about pa, but we may have to have him committed. He's done enough deviltry for one man."

"He has for a fact," Holman agreed. "Well then, I reckon we'll hang and rattle."

Rick walked past the table to the Klein men. "You're fired," he said. "All three of you. I'm helping the sheriff take Wheeler to town. Be out of here before I get back."

"What are you going to do about Klein?" Holman demanded. "He's a son-of-a-bitch when he's mad, and he's sure as hell gonna be sore about this."

"We figure he was back of Hawks' murder," Osmand said, "and we likewise figure he was the one who shot Barney. I'll hold him on suspicion of murder when I find him."

Holman glanced uneasily at the men beside him, then said, "He'll be hard to take, sheriff."

Rick read fear in his tone of voice and in his wrinkled face, and he also sensed the hate that the four old Rainbow hands had for the foreman. He said, "I'm looking for him, Slim. I can't let Barney's shooting go."

"I hope you find him in time," Holman said. "You owe us for what we just done, so keep the bastard off our backs."

"I aim to," Osmand said. "All right, Wheeler. Let's ride."

Later, with their long shadows moving across the snow ahead of them, Rick said in a low tone so Wheeler wouldn't hear, "Sheriff, we were just plain lucky that Klein wasn't in the bunkhouse."

Wheeler rode ahead of them. Osmand stared somberly at his back. He nodded, saying, "We wouldn't be alive if he had been. The man's a devil. His men believe in him and the others are afraid of him." He paused, then asked, "Where do you suppose he is?"

"I don't know," Rick said, "but I don't think he'd go to the Smith place alone. Not after what happened there."

"He's a slick bastard," Osmand said uneasily. "I figure he's up to some shenanigan. We ain't out of the woods till he's in jail or dead."

That, Rick told himself, was a statement he could agree to.

"I've bitched about being too old to be sheriff," Osmand said sourly, "and about being stove up by rheumatiz and not wanting to get out in the cold, but I never really knowed how bad off I was until I tried to get my gun out of leather back there. You were plugging Bean and them other fellows were climbing all over Wheeler and there I was, slow as molasses being poured out of a pitcher on a day like this."

That, too, Rick thought, was a statement he could agree to.

Osmand turned his head to look squarely at Rick. "But by God, I'm gonna see this through to the finish."

CHAPTER 21

Rick rode beside the sheriff with Long John Wheeler still in front of them. The sun was nearly down, and darkness was not far away. The wind had picked up, tossing the snow around and causing it to drift. The air seemed much colder now that the wind was blowing again, and Rick turned the collar of his sheepskin up around his neck. He shivered and rubbed his gloved hands together.

When they reached the bridge where the road turned off to the Smith place, Rick said, "I'll leave you here, sheriff. I guess Ruth will have supper waiting for me."

Osmand reined up and called to Wheeler to wait. He said, "Hold on, Rick."

Osmand cleared his throat, and Rick sensed what was about to happen. He would want Rick to take Wheeler on in with him. Rick told himself that his answer would be no. He'd sided Osmand in the showdown back in the Rainbow bunkhouse. Wasn't that enough?

But as he looked at Osmand and saw the fear and the feeling of inadequacy that was in the old man, his resolution to pull out faded away. Osmand opened his mouth, but the words wouldn't come.

"Go on, Rick," the sheriff said finally. "You've done enough. I can't ask you to do no more."

"You want me to go on into town with you," Rick said. "That it?"

"I'd sure be beholden to you if you would," Osmand said. "I'll feel better when this bastard is locked up."

Rick sighed. He knew he wasn't as cold and miserable as Osmand was. It would be a hell of a note for Wheeler to get the drop on the old man and walk away to join up with Klein.

"All right," Rick said. "I'll go with you."

"Good." Osmand nodded and said to Wheeler, "Get moving."

They rode on to town, the sheriff with his head lowered against the wind. Ruth would worry, Rick knew, but there wasn't anything he could do about it. He hoped they ran into Klein in town. This wouldn't be finished until Klein was finished, and there was always the risk that Klein would hear that Wheeler was jailed and would walk in and take him out at gunpoint. Maybe, as slow and filled with misery as the old man was, it would be the only thing he could do.

Reaching the front of the jail, they reined up and tied. Wheeler glanced at them once as if considering his chances if he made a run for it.

Rick said, "Try it. I'd feel better if you were as dead as Monte Bean."

"I ain't gonna try nothing," Wheeler muttered. "All I want is to get warm."

He walked into the jail ahead of his captors. Osmand struck a match and lighted a bracket lamp, then motioned for Wheeler to go ahead of him into the big cell at the rear of the sheriff's office. Osmand locked the door and turned away.

"Build a fire," Wheeler yelled. "It's as cold in here as it is outside."

Osmand dropped into a chair. "Damn, I'm tired," he said. "You build the fire, Rick. There's kindling yonder in the woodbox."

Osmand was tired enough to be sick, and the thought came to Rick that the old man had just about had enough of the running around. He'd done pretty well today, far better than Rick had expected, but the strain was beginning to take its toll.

"Sure, I'll build it," Rick said.

He took his knife out of his pocket, whittled a handful of shavings from a pine stick, and laid them in the bottom of the heater, then struck a match to them and added pieces of kindling. The wood was dry, and in a matter of minutes it was crackling and snapping so that Rick was able to pile bigger chunks on top of the flames.

"By God, I wish I could stay right here," Osmand said, "and not go outside all night."

"You'd better get your supper and then come back here to sleep," Rick said.

"I reckon so," Osmand agreed. "Ain't much sense in going home and having my wife yak at me for the rest of the night." He shook his head. "I dunno, though. If Klein walks in here and throws a gun on me, I won't have much chance."

"Maybe you'll throw a gun on him," Rick said.

"Maybe, if I'm awake." He rose. "Let's go over to the hotel. I figure Jack Noble will be there. He keeps a room there full-time, for the nights when the stage lays over here. I'm sure we'll find him in the hotel somewhere. I don't reckon he'll be out sashaying around in this kind of weather."

They went outside, mounted, and rode to the hotel. Rick wasn't sure what the sheriff intended to do, but he obviously wanted

Rick's backing. The chances were good the stage driver still wouldn't make a definite identification, and maybe that was why Osmand wanted Rick with him.

Right now Rick was in a mood to make the driver talk and not be very scrupulous about the methods he used. This was something Osmand didn't think he could or should do as long as he was wearing the star.

They strode into the hotel, Osmand turning toward the bar, Rick a step behind him. The driver wasn't there. They wheeled back to the lobby, Osmand striding to the desk.

"You seen Jack Noble lately?" the sheriff asked.

The clerk nodded. "He's in the dining room."

"Thanks," Osmand said, and led the way into the dining room, Rick still close behind.

The stage driver was sitting at a table in the back of the room. Osmand walked directly to him, not stopping until he towered over the man.

"Jack," he said, "I want an identification of the men who took Joe Hawks off the stage. I know damn well you were lying this afternoon and that you know who they were."

The driver scooted his chair back, glancing at Osmand and then at Rick and finally bringing his gaze back to the sheriff. He said, his voice almost a whine, "I don't know who they were and you can't make me sign no statement that I recognized 'em."

"We'll see," Osmand said. "Rick, go to the desk and get a sheet of paper, a pen, and a bottle of ink."

Rick nodded and wheeled away. He threaded his way through the tables and stepped into the lobby. He made his request. The clerk handed him paper, pen, and a bottle of ink. Rick returned to the stage driver's table.

"Here you are, sheriff," Rick said, placing the things on the table in front of Noble. "You think we're gonna have to twist Jack's arm a little bit?"

"Twist and be damned," the driver snapped. "I ain't signing no death warrant. If I done what you're asking, them two bastards would see to it that I didn't live long enough to testify at their trial. If they didn't take care of me, Curly Klein would."

Rick sat down across the table from Noble. "Jack, there are a few facts you'd better know. One, Monte Bean is dead. Two, Long John Wheeler is in jail. Three, we're looking for Klein and we'll arrest him as soon as we find him for the murder of my brother, Barney. We figure Wheeler can tell us something about that, too. Barney ain't dead yet, but he's close to it."

Noble rose. "I'm walking out of here and I ain't signing nothing. I didn't have to tell you as much as I did this afternoon. I'm sorry I opened my mouth."

Osmand grabbed him by the shoulders and jammed him back into his chair. "You ain't walking nowhere till you do your duty as a citizen."

"There's Fact Number Four that I ain't told you," Rick said. "We're stomping a bunch of snakes today and we're not letting up until we finish. We need this identification. Once we get it, we'll work on Wheeler till he spills the beans on Klein."

"Klein's a killer," Noble said in a low tone. "You know it as well as I do, and right now he's a free man."

"Fact Number Four is that I'm a killer, too," Rick said, "and if I have to add you to my list, I sure as hell will."

Noble snorted. "Who'd you ever kill, boy?"

"Scott and Monte Bean," Rick answered.

"The hell!" Noble turned to Osmand. "Is he lying?"

"He killed 'em all right," Osmand said

grimly. "He's my unofficial deputy. If it hadn't been for him, I'd be dead and Long John Wheeler wouldn't be in jail."

Noble thought about it a minute, then shook his head. "I know what Klein is. I ain't that sure about a kid who ain't been shaving more'n a few months."

Rick leaned forward, anger boiling up in him. He said slowly, "Jack, the part of Fact Number Four that's important is that this whole business hits me and my brother and my mother. I ain't sure yet how pa's gonna wind up, but he's in it, too. I don't figure on going on living the way we have been. We're clearing it up tonight if we find Klein. I wouldn't want to shoot you in the guts, but if you keep on being bull-headed, I will."

For a moment there was only silence. No one else in the dining room said a word or even moved. Then the ominous click of a gun being cocked could be heard throughout the room. Sweat broke through Noble's skin and a muscle in his cheek began to jump. "You wouldn't shoot me in cold blood, Rick. I know you too well —"

Rick squeezed the trigger, the bullet driving into the floor at Noble's feet. The sound was like a cannon in the confines of the dining room, and it drove Noble against the back of his chair; he fell out of it and sprawled on the floor as powder smoke eddied out from under the table.

He stared at Rick as if he had never seen him before. He licked his lips, his face turning so white that Rick thought he was going to faint. He whispered, "By God, I believe you'd do it." He pulled himself to his feet and sat down. He began to write, his hand trembling so much that it was difficult to read what he had written.

Noble signed his name and showed the sheet to Osmand. "Satisfied?"

The sheriff nodded.

Rick rose and holstered his gun. "I'll get along," he said.

Osmand nodded and held out his hand. "Saying thanks ain't enough, but it's all I can say."

"It's enough," Rick said as he shook hands. "I'll be at Smith's ranch if you need me."

He walked out of the dining room without glancing at the trembling stage driver. Crossing the lobby, he stepped out into the chilly, wind-swept street. Mounting, he took the road to Smith's Rafter S.

Chapter 22

By the time Rick reached the Smith place, the wind had increased until it had created what was close to a ground blizzard. He could not see the house or barn until he was actually between them. He turned into the barn, off-saddled, and led the horse into a stall. He forked hay into the manger, then, head down, crossed to the house.

He knocked on the door, slapping his hat against his leg to knock off the snow as he yelled out his identification. Apparently Milt Smith heard him above the wind because he opened the door and Rick slid into the house.

Smith shut the door as Rick wiped his boots on a rug that Ruth had left on the floor near the door and hung up his hat and sheepskin. Ruth was in the kitchen. Hearing the door slam, she ran into the front room.

"Rick," Ruth cried. "Where have you been and what have you been doing? I've been

223

worried."

She ran to him. He hugged and kissed her, lifting her off the floor until she told him to put her down. "I've been busy, I'm cold, and I'm hungry. What can you do about it?"

"I can't do anything about you being busy," she said, "but we've got a good fire going in both stoves, so you'll soon get warm, and I kept your supper hot. Come on. I'll dish it up."

She took his hand and led him into the kitchen. Milt followed hesitantly as if he wasn't sure he should be in his own kitchen. He had changed during the last few hours, Rick thought. He was no longer the tough, self-confident man that Rick had known most of his life. He had barred the front door before he left the living room, and now he crossed to the back door and examined the bar to see that it was in place, probably for about the tenth time, Rick told himself.

"We didn't wait," Ruth said apologetically. "We didn't know what time you'd be back and I thought we'd better eat while Barney is sleeping. He's a lot better, Rick. His color is good and he's breathing evenly."

"He hasn't come around?" Rick asked.

"Well, yes, he did for a minute or two," Ruth said as she poured Rick's coffee. "I'm not sure whether he was out of his head or not, but he recognized me. I sat beside his bed for a little while holding his hand. He kept trying to tell me something about Klein wanting to kill a man named Joe Hawks. That mean anything to you?"

Rick nodded. "Yeah, it means something, all right. We know about it, but Barney's testimony will be that much more if Klein comes to trial. We haven't found him, but we will. He didn't kill Hawks himself, but he ordered it. We've got Long John Wheeler in jail and Monte Bean is dead. He resisted arrest."

Milt Smith sat down across the table from Rick and filled and lighted his pipe. "Tell us what happened after you left here," he said.

Rick told them his story between mouthfuls of Ruth's delicious home cooking.

Smith took his pipe out of his mouth and stared at it for a moment. Finally he said, "Well, it looks to me like Klein and your pa got their claws clipped purty good, but we ain't out of the woods yet."

Rick nodded agreement. "As long as Klein's alive and out of jail, it's like having a two-ton rock hanging over your head, ready to drop." He sipped his coffee, then added, "Milt, nobody can do anything with pa. I'm sure of that. Once we get Klein out of the way, we'll see what it takes to have pa committed. It's the only answer. Nobody but a man like Klein could work with him the way he is now. I'm going to run Rainbow and I'll hire back all the old hands I can find, but we've got to take care of pa so he can't make any more foolish decisions."

Ruth put her arms around Rick's shoulders. "I didn't think the sheriff would make you help him fight."

"I didn't, either," Rick said, "but I was the only help he had, and he knew he couldn't hack it by himself. At least we'll have some help putting pa away. I mean, with Osmand's and Doc Doan's advice, I think we can do it. Judge Callahan is the one I ain't sure about." He shook his head. "I'm worried about ma, too. She won't leave Rainbow."

Smith held up his hand and turned his head to listen. He asked, "Hear anything?"

Rick and Ruth were silent, listening. A faint cry came to them from outside, probably from the front of the house, Rick thought. He said, "Somebody's out there, all right. I'll go see."

"Might be a trap," Smith said uneasily. "Maybe Klein's just trying to get the door open."

"Grab your shotgun," Rick said. "If it is a trap, you can be ready."

He went to the front room, put on his hat and sheepskin, then opened the door and moved outside quickly. No one was close. He said, "Shut the door." Smith obeyed. For a moment Rick stood motionless, staring into the darkness and listening. For a time he heard nothing except the wind. Then the cry came again, a weak cry as if the man was so exhausted he couldn't shout any longer.

Rick considered the possibility that Smith had been right, that Klein was out there hoping to get the door open, or would lure Rick outside and shoot him on sight. He discarded the suspicion, partly because he didn't think it would be Klein's way of getting at him, but mostly because he couldn't bring himself to turn his back on anyone who was out there in the wind and who was as far gone as this man seemed to be.

Rick answered the yell and started to run in the direction he thought it came from. A short time later he made out the vague form of a horse ahead of him. He heard the cry again. Another dozen strides brought him to the horse. A man was in the saddle slumped over the horn.

Rick led the horse to the front door of the house, shouting for Smith to open up as he pulled the man out of the saddle. He carried him inside, Smith shutting and barring the door behind him. It was not until he laid the man on the couch that he saw it was Judge Callahan.

Smith swore softly. "Now what'd fetch an old goat like him out on a night like this?"

"Dunno," Rick said, "but I'm betting Klein had something to do with it. I'm going back out and put his horse in the barn."

He led the horse across the yard, put him into a stall and tied him, then pulled off the saddle and fed him. He rubbed the horse down, thinking that it must have taken a lot of pressure of some kind to force Callahan into making the ride from town.

When he returned to the house, he found Callahan sitting close to the heater, his thin, liver-spotted hands extended over it. He was shivering violently, but it was his gray color that shocked Rick. He looked like a dead man.

Ruth brought him a cup of coffee spiked with whiskey. His hands were trembling so violently he spilled more than he drank.

Another ten minutes passed before Callahan could talk. Finally, he said, "Don't tell me I'm a damned fool for being out on a night like this, but I will tell you I'm a coward or I wouldn't have listened to Klein. He sent me out here.

"The wind had let up some and I made it pretty good until I turned at the bridge, and then the wind came up harder than ever and kicked up so much snow I didn't know where I was. I thought I was going to freeze to death before Rick carried me in here. I didn't know how close I was to your house, Milt, so I just stopped and yelled, figuring that somebody might hear me."

He wiped a hand across his face and shook his head. "I thought I was a goner. I got to thinking about my misbegotten life and how I'd helped Jay Proctor with his schemes, and how I'd listened to Klein because I figured he was going to be top dog and I wanted to be on his side. Besides, I was scared not to do what he said. Well, I had a good, long look at myself, and I figured I was dying in the storm and headed right for hell. I'm ashamed of myself, Rick. By God, I'm ashamed."

"Why did Klein send you out here?" Rick asked.

"To lie to you so he could kill you," Callahan answered. "I was supposed to tell you that I'd been to Rainbow and your pa had had a change of heart and wanted to see you right away. Klein figured you'd head out for Rainbow and he'd be there waiting to put a slug into you as soon as you showed up.

"Well, I intended to do what he wanted until I got lost and figured I was dying. That's when I realized how stupid I'd been. I swore that if I got out of this alive, I'd be a changed man."

He hadn't been rational, and Rick wasn't sure he was now. He certainly didn't believe that Callahan would stay changed once he got over his scare. But he did believe Callahan's story. Klein would be waiting for him at Rainbow.

Rick put on his coat and hat.

Ruth cried, "Rick, you're not as crazy as I think you are. You couldn't be. You're not going to Rainbow?"

"That's exactly where I'm going." Rick said. "I'm taking ma somewhere even if I have to hog-tie her and carry her out of the house."

"Bring her here," Ruth said as if she knew there was no use to argue with him.

"I'll do that," he said, and left the house.

CHAPTER 23

The weather was often capricious this time of year, so Rick was not surprised to find that the wind had died down, that the sky was clear and the air warmer than it had been when he'd ridden from town.

He saddled up and started toward Rainbow, not sure what he would do when he arrived. Klein would have set up some sort of trap. Rick was sure he was not a man who would give him a fair fight at a time like this. Besides, he had practically told Callahan he planned to bushwhack Rick. The problem, then, was to guess where he'd set his trap.

Rick could think of several places where Klein wouldn't be. The bunkhouse was one. He wouldn't take a chance on Rainbow's old hands siding with Rick. Probably not the house. He wouldn't want Jay to see his son gunned down. Besides, Rick's mother was there to witness what happened. He might wind up killing her, too, but Rick thought that Klein was man enough not to kill a woman.

That left the stable and the corrals, and Rick decided it would probably be the stable. This seemed a good guess because he would have to put his horse up before he went into the house, as though he did not suspect a trap, and Klein had no reason to think that he did.

Lights in the ranch house appeared in the darkness ahead of him. His father was still sitting there at the window just as he had all day, Rick guessed. A few minutes later he saw that there was also a light in the stable, and the door was open. This was not unusual on nights when there were a good many things going on. Klein would assume that Rick believed he was expected and was even being welcomed; he would lead his horse into the runway, and Klein would smoke him down before he had a chance to draw his gun.

Rick pulled off the road and circled the house. He left his horse behind one of the outbuildings. Moving slowly and silently, he eased toward the stable door. He flexed his right hand, and for the first time, felt fear work into him.

He had heard Klein brag about his gunfights and the number of men he had killed. He believed the stories because in most ways Klein was not a braggart. Rick wouldn't be fighting a man like Scott Shell or Monte Bean. Klein was the best of the lot.

Reaching the corner of the barn, Rick paused, thinking the odds were good that Klein was in the stable expecting to see or hear Rick ride up. Rick's only chance, then, depended on surprising the man. A little luck wouldn't hurt either, Rick thought.

He eased along the wall, listening to the deadly silence. He was probably late by Klein's reckoning. Rick paused ten feet from the stable door and waited, not sure what his next move would be. If he walked through that door, Klein would kill him before he had a chance to pull the trigger.

The minutes dragged by. Then Rick's heart bounced into his throat. Klein was there all right. He was getting impatient, Rick guessed. Apparently he had come to the door for a better look, but he never stepped through it, so Rick had only a glimpse of his long shadow thrown by the overhead lantern into the snow. He stepped back immediately, perhaps thinking that Rick might be close enough to see him. Rick had dropped his hand to his gun but now released his grip on the cedar butt, convinced that he had to figure out a way to go in after Klein.

The main part of the barn was the hay mow and a series of granaries along the inside wall that ran parallel to the row of mangers in the stable. It would be dark as a cave, but Rick had spent hours playing there as a boy and later pitching hay and emptying oat-sacks into the granaries, so he knew the interior of the barn as well as he knew his own room at home.

He moved to the back door opposite where Klein stood. The trick would be to get in without Klein hearing him. He opened the door, slid inside, and pulled the door shut as quickly as he could. The squeak of the hinges seemed inordinately loud to him, but he figured he was too far away for Klein to hear.

Rick remained there several seconds; then, confident that Klein had not heard him, he moved along the wall that was the front of the granaries. He paused again and listened. Still hearing nothing from the stable, he continued until he reached the hall that led to the mangers.

Here he could see a faint gleam of light from the lantern in the runway. He could make out a manger and an empty stall directly ahead of him. He slipped forward, the litter on the floor muffling any sound his boots would have made. He eased silently over the manger into the stall. He could not see Klein from here, but he was convinced that the man was in the runway somewhere between this stall and the stable door.

Rick had kept himself under strict control up to this moment, but now he was unable to hold a tight rein any longer. He drew his gun and lunged into the runway. "Klein!" he shouted.

He had guessed right. Curly Klein stood at the far end of the runway facing the door. He wheeled, drawing his gun as he turned, and fired at almost the same instant Rick did. Almost, but not quite. The two reports rolled out together, making one continuous echoing roar.

Klein staggered under the impact of Rick's slug. His bullet, a fraction of a hair off course, whizzed past Rick's left shoulder. Klein's left hand went out against the wall beside him. For a moment he held himself there, his gun dropping from his hand; then his huge body gave way, and he sprawled into the straw and manure on the runway floor.

Rick walked toward him, still holding his

smoking gun. He looked down at Klein and heard him whisper, "You goddamn lucky kid." That was all. He died that way, lying on his back in the litter of the stable floor, his hat falling off his head, his gun butt inches from his outflung hand.

Men rushed out of the bunkhouse and raced toward the stable. Slim Holman was in the lead. When they saw who was standing and who was on the floor, they were stopped dead in their tracks. A sigh of relief could be heard from the crowd.

"We figured it was you, boy," Holman said. "The three Klein men pulled their freight awhile ago. Klein came in looking for 'em, and when he heard what had happened, I thought he was gonna go up in smoke."

"Monte Bean's body still here?" Rick asked.

He was shaking now that it was over. He holstered his gun and moved back along the runway, not wanting the men to see the fear on his face.

Holman answered. "Yeah, we rolled it in canvas and laid it in the other end of the barn."

"Harness up a team and haul both of them into town," Rick said. "Unload 'em at Doc's place and notify the sheriff."

They hesitated, staring at Rick as if they considered the order unreasonable at this time of night.

Rick said, "Come on. You sure ain't worked very hard since the storm started. And if you see any of the old hands around town, tell 'em their old job is waiting for 'em."

Holman shrugged his shoulders, grinned, and said, "Sure, boss."

Rick strode past them out of the stable and crossed the yard to the house. He paused on the porch long enough to knock the snow from his boots, then opened the door and stepped into the front room. Jay sat in his chair facing the window just as Rick had guessed he would, his revolver on his lap.

"You can go to bed now, pa," Rick said. "There will be no raid on the Rafter S. I just shot and killed Curly Klein. He was waiting in the stable to bushwhack me. The hands are bringing his body to the sheriff's place, I'm hiring back the old crew, now that Klein and his outlaws are gone. Barney's alive and I think he's going to make it. We won't have no more trouble working Rainbow now."

Jay turned his head and stared at Rick as he listened. He might have been a sane man before Rick came in, but now as he grasped what Rick said, his eyes took on that wild expression Rick had seen before.

"You liar!" he screamed. "Barney's dead. Curly told me Barney was dead. Curly never lied to me. It's you that's lying." He choked; he began to tremble as his face turned red and then purple.

"No, I'm not lying," Rick said. "Barney's at the Smith place. He came out of it this afternoon long enough to tell Ruth that Klein was figuring on murdering Joe Hawks. But Barney was too late. Klein had Hawks killed before we could do anything about it."

"Lies," Jay screamed. "All lies!" Suddenly, without warning, he gripped the butt of his gun, lifted it from his lap, and aimed the barrel at Rick. Rick froze in his tracks.

"Don't do it, Jay," Mary Proctor called from the kitchen doorway. Even as crazy as Jay Proctor was, Rick had not believed he was capable of killing his own son. But now he read death in his father's distorted face, in the wild expression in his eyes. To his own surprise, Rick discovered that for the first time he could not draw his own gun to defend himself. Not against his own father.

The hammer of the big gun was back. Sweat broke through Rick's skin and ran down his face. The seconds dragged out to an eternity as he told himself he should not have gone at it this way. Any other way would have been better than what he had done.

He thought of his mother, of Ruth, of Rainbow, and of how much he was needed. He heard the gunshot, but it was not the roar of Jay's heavy .45 that he had expected.

Slowly Jay's head tipped forward, his fingers went slack, and the .45 crashed against the wooden floor. Rick looked at his mother as she stood in the kitchen doorway, her small revolver in her hand, a faint dribble of smoke rising from the muzzle.

"I guess I've always known that someday I'd have to do this," she said slowly and without expression.

Rick went to her, put his arm around her, and led her back into the kitchen.

"You could have killed him," she said. "You had time."

"No, I couldn't," he said. "I used to think I could. I've dreamed about killing him, but when the time came, I couldn't do it."

Tears began wetting her cheeks. "He didn't used to be this way, Rick. There was a time when he was a — a normal man."

"Put on your coat, ma," Rick said. "I'm taking you to the Rafter S. The last thing

Ruth said when I left was for me to bring you back."

She nodded, and without another word, took her coat off a nail near the back door and put it on. They went out together.

The nightmare was over.

We hope you have enjoyed this Large Print book. Other Thorndike, Wheeler, Kennebec, and Chivers Press Large Print books are available at your library or directly from the publishers.

For information about current and upcoming titles, please call or write, without obligation, to:

Publisher
Thorndike Press
10 Water St., Suite 310
Waterville, ME 04901
Tel. (800) 223-1244

or visit our Web site at:

http://gale.cengage.com/thorndike

OR

Chivers Large Print
published by AudioGO Ltd
St James House, The Square
Lower Bristol Road
Bath BA2 3BH
England
Tel. +44(0) 800 136919
info@audiogo.co.uk
www.audiogo.co.uk

All our Large Print titles are designed for easy reading, and all our books are made to last.